D0915575

Trans-Atlantyk

Witold Gombrowicz

Translated by Carolyn French and Nina Karsov

Introduction by Stanislaw Baranczak

Yale University Press ~ New Haven and London

The publication of this book is supported by a grant from the Legion of Young Polish Women.

Designed by Rebecca Gibb.
Set in Bauer Bodoni type by The Composing Room of Michigan, Inc.
Printed in the United States of America by Vail-Ballou Press, Binghamton, New York.

Library of Congress Cataloging-in-Publication Data

Gombrowicz, Witold.
[Trans-Atlantyk. English]
Trans-Atlantyk / Witold Gombrowicz; translated by Carolyn French and Nina Karsov; introduction by Stanislaw Baranczak.
p. cm.
ISBN 0-300-05384-3.
I. Title.
PG7158.G669T713 1994.
891.8′537—dc20 93-11880 CIP

A catalogue record for this book is available from the British Library.

The paper in this book meets the guidelines for permanence and durability of the Committee on Production Guidelines for Book Longevity of the Council on Library Resources.

10 9 8 7 6 5 4 3 2 1

This translation is dedicated to Szymon Szechter,
without whose encouragement we would not have persisted.

Contents

Introduction

A masterpiece of twentieth-century fiction and one of the most dazzlingly original works in all of Polish literature, *Trans-Atlantyk* would not exist had its author declined an offer to spend a few leisurely weeks aboard a pleasure boat. Almost exactly forty years have passed since the first Polish-language edition of this Argentinian novel by a Polish writer came out—as if to make its own geographic unorthodoxy even more perplexing—in Paris. Many of its readers have probably reflected on how the emergence of even the most accomplished work of a writer of genius may depend not so much on his or her creative intent as on an utterly trivial twist of fate.

In the case of Witold Gombrowicz, it was not a single accident but rather a random coincidence that made the creation of his masterpiece possible, albeit fourteen years after the voyage that inspired it. Gombrowicz's disembarcation in Buenos Aires on August 21, 1939, and the Nazi invasion of his homeland eleven days later recall the "twin halves of one august event" in Thomas Hardy's "The Convergence of the Twain"—another masterpiece having to do with transatlantic liners. That *Trans-Atlantyk* was born from the marriage of something as grand as world war and something as minuscule as the author's ocean cruise does, however, have its own peculiar logic. These two unequal events have one thing in common: the ironic discrepancy between the individual's aspirations and the burden of obligations that ethnicity, national tradition, and one's chosen profession put upon one's shoulders. Both Gombrowicz and the novel's narrator (who bears Gombrowicz's name) are concerned with the supra-individual notion of being a Pole or, more specifically, a Polish writer.

The transatlantic travel was not just a pleasure cruise: Gombrowicz the real-life author (Gombrowicz the narrator does not reveal much on this account) was invited abroad, all expenses paid, for a specific purpose. The trip was the maiden voyage of the ocean liner *Bolesław Chrobry*, named after the first king of Poland in the eleventh century. Gombrowicz, along with another young author, Czesław Straszewicz, was expected to represent (in particular to the sizable Polish émigré community in Argentina) the culture of the Polish Republic, reborn in 1918 as a result of the world war. In the novel, as soon as the news of the German-Polish hostilities reaches Argentina, the expectations of Gombrowicz's compatriots change: instead of fulfilling his mission as an informal cultural envoy he is supposed to rush back home, arms in hand, to defend Poland against the enemy. Yet Gombrowicz, a sort of human synecdoche, is still expected to function as part of a whole, as a representative of something larger than himself: his nation, its indomitable spirit, and its literature's traditional role of making this spirit even more indomitable.

Gombrowicz the narrator refuses to comply, despite his casual acceptance of the peace-time "mission" (which, we may surmise, was just a convenient excuse to take a vacation abroad at the government's expense). His one-person mutiny may, of course, be attributed by some to simple cowardice, by others to an abhorrence of the essentially senseless bloodbath of war. Yet the truth is more complex. What Gombrowicz the narrator refuses to suffer any more—taking the dramatic yes-or-no question of his return as an opportunity to make a clean break with his half-hearted compliance—is the overwhelming power of stereotype, of What Is Expected from You, of (to use the term that Gombrowicz adopted in his essays and diary) Form.

American readers of Gombrowicz's *Diary* will be familiar with this term, which denotes one of the two opposed pillars of his philosophy. Probably no other fiction writer in modern world literature can match the almost intimidating consistency and precision of Gombrowicz's system of ideas. The words *philosophy* and *system* contain no exaggeration: *Gombrowicz the Philosopher*, a selection of his essays published a few years ago in Poland, attests to the utmost seriousness and orderliness of the intellect of this seemingly whimsical and nonsensical writer.

The central and most original component of Gombrowicz's system is his vision of what he calls the "interhuman church." This slightly puzzling term embraces the entirety of more or less ritualized or institutionalized (hence the metaphor of "church") relationships binding—and/or pitting against each other—the individual and "others" (both other individuals and society as a whole). According to Gombrowicz, by virtue of being human each of us is doomed to be part of the "interhuman church": leaving it would be tantamount to renouncing one's humanity. Specific individuals' relations to others may, however, vary widely, stretching from a tendency to comply with the prevailing stereotype of behavior to a striving for independence, spontaneity, and freedom.

The individual is, in other words, suspended between the external ideas of Form and Chaos, between total subordination of the ego to the generally accepted patterns of behavior, logic, language, and so forth, and total liberation from all that is inherited or imitated. If this dialectical dualism of Gombrowicz's thought proved so productive as the generating mechanism of each of his short stories, plays, and novels, it is for one reason: neither the extreme of Form nor that of Chaos is accepted unequivocally as a positive solution for the dilemma of human existence.

Such an acceptance can never happen in Gombrowicz, since he is fully aware that both Form and Chaos have disadvantages as well as advantages. Compliance to Form gives us something to lean on in our attempts to fit into this or that human community or group; by adopting that which is commonly shared within such a group, we gain access to its repertory of symbols, and that in turn enables us to communicate with others and to confirm our existence by means of its reflection in others' eyes. On the other hand, the same Form that enables the individual psyche to express itself is also the psyche's chief *obstacle* to expressing itself. By imposing on us ready-made "languages" of generally recognizable, therefore more or less repetitive and trite, symbols, Form in fact distorts as much as it grants, in extreme cases making it impossible for us to communicate anything spontaneously and freely. To reverse this equation, attaining the extreme of Chaos would allow us to be completely spontaneous, free, and sincere in whatever we try to communicate, but then the very process of communication would not occur, since a complete absence of Form would entail the lack of any "language" common to us and the others. Striving for Form, we gain acceptance of others but lose our individual uniqueness; letting ourselves sink into Chaos, we remain individually unique all right, but others cannot comprehend and accept us. In fact, complete identification of the individual with the extreme of Form would mean dissolution in the conventional, that is, spiritual death; complete identification with the extreme of Chaos would mean absolute isolation, that is, spiritual death again.

Both extremes—instead of Form versus Chaos, we might speak of perfection versus freedom—remain, therefore, equally unattainable. This realization is part of the genius of Gombrowicz. He never let himself be fooled by the two most popular fallacies of the past two centuries concerning the relationship between the individual and society: the romantic claim that only the individual's total self-liberation from society's constraints is worth living for, and the positivistic or, especially, Marxist illusion that human beings can be defined completely in terms of their social roles. It is not just the consistency of his philosophical system that makes Gombrowicz a great writer; it is, rather, his ability to discern and expose the same

fundamental antinomy in a number of apparently different kinds of interhuman relationships. In his literary works, the opposition of Form and Chaos or perfection and freedom takes on many shapes depending on which particular social hierarchies are scrutinized. Form versus Chaos can thus be translated into oppositions of age (maturity/immaturity), social class (aristocrats/plebeians), civilizational tradition (West/East), cultural background (elitist/mass culture), and even sexual persuasion ("accepted" heterosexuality/"ostracized" homosexuality). Superiority versus inferiority would be another pair of synonyms housing diverse oppositions under its roof—that is, if we keep in mind that superiority may take on, ironically, the shape of constraining uniformity, whereas inferiority may appear darkly attractive because of the chance of liberation it seems to offer to the individual.

Gombrowicz's slim oeuvre may contain novels such as *Ferdydurke* whose revelatory impact was much stronger than *Trans-Atlantyk*'s, or which hit a higher notch on an imaginary scale of philosophical complexity, such as *Kosmos;* however, it is not only my opinion that *Trans-Atlantyk* represents his greatest accomplishment as an artist. Although this novel, his second (if we are to omit his serialized gothic parody *Opętani* [The possessed], the publication of which in a Warsaw tabloid had been interrupted by the outbreak of war), is his shortest, it took the longest time to write. Begun in 1948, it appeared only in 1953, sixteen years after *Ferdydurke*. To be sure, Gombrowicz did not spend all of that time chiseling *Trans-Atlantyk*'s fine points. During most of the war and postwar years he was reduced to struggling for survival, coping with extreme poverty and wasting his energies on a job as a bank clerk offered to him by a Polish banker in Buenos Aires. According to Gombrowicz, he wrote *Trans-Atlantyk* on his desk at the bank, hiding the manuscript in a drawer whenever his superior entered the room.

Great as Gombrowicz's earlier and later novels are, *Trans-Atlantyk* surpasses them, I think, in at least four essential respects. First, its plot, for all its absurdly unexpected twists and downright fantastic developments, stems consistently from the initial premise, the fictitious version of the author's momentous decision to stay in Argentina—the single most dramatic event in his life. The first words of the novel, "I feel a need to relate here . . . ," are already charged with the urgency that spurs the narrative momentum of the ensuing paragraphs and chapters. As a result, even though no one would be naive enough to take Gombrowicz the narrator for a mirror-reflection of Gombrowicz the author, or the former's wildly spun tall tale for the latter's genuine and accurate confession, the fact remains that this novel, perhaps the most grotesquely fantastic ever written in Polish, is also the most personal and engaging of all Gombrowicz's works of fiction.

Second, the urgency that marks the narrator's "need to relate" his story translates felicitously into the elusive quality of *Trans-Atlantyk*'s style and composition.This quality might be described as a combination of extreme speed with highly precise rhythmic organization. The latter is felt on all levels of this freely moving yet carefully choreographed work, from phonetics (for instance, devices such as alliteration) to syntax (contrasting long and short sentences, dramatic use of the historical present tense, and so on) to the composition of paragraphs and chapters (the refrainlike repetitions of certain key words or phrases). With the possible exception of Gombrowicz's play *Operetta*, there is no other work in his entire output which, for all its deliberately jarring notes, is so firmly based on musical principles of composition and which, for all its deliberate tripping over its own feet, rushes forward with such an irresistible dancelike aplomb.

Third, *Trans-Atlantyk* is the most memorably compact among Gombrowicz's fictional embodiments of his recurrent system of ideas. What might be called the objective correlatives of his philosophy—fictional plots, situations, characters and their mutual relationships incarnating this or that specific variant of "the interhuman church"—are no less admirably inventive in most of his other works. Here, however, several such variants come together to form a kind of musical chord characterized by extraordinarily com-

plex harmony. In *Ferdydurke*, for example, three different locales, milieus, and corresponding stages of the plot (the narrator's adventures at school, in Mr. and Mrs. Youthful's house, and in the country estate) had to be presented consecutively, in a linear sequence, as three different versions of the Form-versus-Chaos conflict. The innovation of *Trans-Atlantyk* is that Gombrowicz puts several manifestations of the same conflict together and makes them resound simultaneously, in a polyphonic composition reminiscent of a Baroque fugue.

This is mostly possible thanks to the power with which the plot's point of departure—the narrator's decision to stay in Argentina—continues to weigh on everything that happens afterwards. This decision to accept the in-between status of a quasi-deserter and would-be immigrant, never at home either among the Poles or among the Argentinians, results in the radical clash of opposites within the narrator's mind and in his immediate surroundings. From that point on, continuously pulled by antithetical values of various sorts and never able to attain either of the two extremes, he can only be a double outcast who strives in vain for an unequivocal identity. Reduced to being a function of what others see in him, the narrator finds himself stretched insufferably between the opposing forces—ethnic, historic, geographic, social, cultural, sexual—to which his new status exposes him. A reluctant performer of several preprogramed roles at once, he is soon entangled in so many different contexts and challenged by so many stereotypes that Gombrowicz the author does not have to lead his protagonist/narrator through changing settings and milieus, as he did in *Ferdydurke.* Once the cast of characters has been introduced (in particular, the father-and-son pair of Tomasz and Ignac, the Argentinian homosexual millionaire Gonzalo, the Baron-Pyckal-Ciumkała trio, and the staff of the Polish embassy), the opposition of Form and Chaos primarily takes on the shape of *Ojczyzna* versus *Synczyzna* (literally, "Fatherland" versus "Sonland," in this translation rendered felicitously as "Patria" and "Filistria"); but this single antimony is just a shorthand for many others.

Fourth, the ingenious polyphony of *Trans-Atlantyk* owes its striking effect to Gombrowicz's use of stylization. A work of art achieves true greatness when the author invents a crucial device and utilizes it so magnificently that no one can successfully imitate it later. This is precisely what happens in *Trans-Atlantyk*. Gombrowicz's chief stroke of genius while planning the novel was his choice of the specific style to imitate—a style which, one imagines, initially must have sounded bizarre even to him. The story of the twentieth-century Polish writer defecting to Argentina in the first days of the Second World War was to be told, from first to last, in a language and style typical of the seventeenth- and eighteenth-century Polish country squire. *Trans-Atlantyk* was to adopt the generic principles of the Baroque nobleman's oral tale, known in the Polish tradition as *gawęda*.

Not just an aura of anachronism but a set of specific historic, social, and cultural connotations are immediately brought into play by the writer who makes use of this particular convention. Gawęda was a genre characteristic of the culture of provincial gentry at the time when Poland—as a result of the devastating wars that raged all over its territory throughout the seventeenth century—entered a prolonged cultural decline in the early 1700s. One legacy of the Baroque era was Polish literature's profound split between the Westernized model, which flourished mostly at the royal and aristocratic courts, and the so-called Sarmatian model, which found its refuges in thousands of provincial noblemen's manors. The literature that those country squires produced, mostly for their own or their neighbors' entertainment, starting in the early 1600s, was (with a few notable exceptions) more local, parochial, conservative, narrow-minded, and artistically primitive than the writings of the well-educated and cosmopolitan court poets. It had its own strengths, though, which allowed it to survive the tough times; and of all the Sarmatian genres the gawęda in particular proved extraordinarily durable. Although gawęda was occasionally committed to paper and even published, it remained primarily an oral genre, partly because of the deterioration of printing in Poland

during the late seventeenth and early eighteenth centuries, and partly because of the migration of cultural life from the war-ravaged cities to the provinces. The existence of gawęda was supported by its stable social context. As a rule it was listened to rather than read, most typically at convivial gatherings of gentry neighbors on the occasion of a wedding or funeral, on holidays, and so forth.

As such, gawęda is characterized not only by its generally oral or quasi-oral style (hence its colloquial vocabulary, its dynamic, free-flowing, but often convoluted syntax, and its rich use of auditory—that is, phonetic, rhythmic, and inflectional—features of speech) and by its reproduction of the authentic oratory patterns of the typical nobleman from the old Polish-Lithuanian Commonwealth (hence frequent Latinisms, ornate flourishes, and the lavish use of rhetorical devices), but also by its specific audience. The fact that such a tale was, for all its oratory, performed in front of a small group of listeners in domestic circumstances gave gawęda a certain homespun, nonprofessional, but also personal and intimate tone. The fact that the listeners were, as a rule, well-disposed friends, neighbors, and family members representing the same social class, educational background, and cultural taste resulted in the characteristically shorthandlike quality of the narrative, which could easily do without laborious introductions, aside explanations, and detailed references, since the audience knew all there was to know anyway. On the other hand, the fact that every gawęda was supposed to exist first and foremost as an oral performance was intrinsic to its composition: since the narrator performed live, the tale must never slow down or get overgrown with tiring details. Not unlike the present-day stand-up comedian, the typical *gawędziarz* realized that a single yawn in the audience could be his undoing. Therefore, his listeners had to be bombarded by a continuous barrage of flowery expressions, vivid images, dramatically presented scenes, sensational facts, intriguing suspense effects, and rhetorical devices aimed at maintaining contact with the audience or reviving its flagging interest.

The above-mentioned features conspired to create the immediately recognizable style of the gawęda—a style so potent, by the way, that it tended to spread and engulf other narrative genres, sometimes producing interesting hybrids. The title of the famous *Memoirs* of the seventeenth-century nobleman Jan Chryzostom Pasek, for instance, is only partly justified: even though the narrator mostly looks back into the past, he nonetheless shares his reminiscences with the reader in the characteristic gawęda style, one as colloquial and spontaneous as if he were describing events actually taking place in his presence.

In the beginning of the nineteenth century the vicissitudes of Polish political history added another twist to the gawęda's popularity: after the third, and final, partition of Poland among the neighboring powers in 1795, gawęda came to symbolize for many writers what was most original, unique, and, for all its parochial obscurantism, endearing in the traditional Sarmatian culture. Nostalgia for the sunk Atlantis of Poland's provincial gentry resulted not only in a renewed interest in the works of Pasek and other old Polish gawędziarze, but also in imitations and pastiches that offered the illusion of retrieving the lost world by recreating its literary style.

One minor and one major masterpiece of Polish literature emerged in the 1830s as a result of the gawęda's association with this conservative utopia. Written in 1830–32, Henryk Rzewuski's *Pamiątki Soplicy* (Soplica's reminiscences) brilliantly imitates the gawęda style to create a vivid, panoramic, and in some ways disturbing portrayal of gentry life. (Soplica, the narrator/protagonist of this sequence of tales, is a fictitious nobleman with connections at the court of the powerful real-life magnate Radziwiłł.) To Rzewuski's credit, his ultraconservative opinions did not prevent him from offering, through his naively apologetic and blindly self-assured narrator, a sobering account of the ills that had brought old Poland to ruin.

Rzewuski's collection occupies a special niche in Polish literary history on the strength of having been one of a few books that inspired Adam Mickiewicz to create the epic poem *Pan Ta-*

deusz (1834), arguably the most famous literary work in the Polish language. Dubbed "the Bible of Polishness" by a modern critic, *Pan Tadeusz* is a nostalgic yet warmly ironic portrayal of life in a gentry manor in the depths of the Lithuanian woods on the eve of Napoleon's Russian campaign. It was written and published in exile, in the same Paris where, about 120 years later, the novel of another exile, this one living in Argentina, brought the sequence of the gawęda's literary reincarnations to its triumphant yet highly self-ironic conclusion.

Thus sketched, the literary tradition that stretches from Pasek to Gombrowicz reveals one regularity: each new phase of the gawęda's transformation increases the ironic distance between narrator and author. In Pasek, the author *was* the narrator: all the beliefs that the narrator of *Memoirs* stands for and all the opinions he expresses are without doubt those of Pasek himself. A distinct hiatus appears in Rzewuski, who, however, does little more than distance himself from his narrator, letting him speak and freely reveal his mind's characteristic idiosyncrasies, limitations, and biases. Mickiewicz goes one step farther: he also employs a naive narrator, but the implied presence of his own beliefs and opinions manifests itself in numerous subtle yet unmistakable ways, through the varying degrees of irony with which he treats the narrator.

Gombrowicz, at first glance, seems to have returned to Pasek's old ways: does not his narrator bear the name of Witold Gombrowicz? Is he not going, at least initially, through the experiences that, to the best of our knowledge, the author himself went through in real life? This, however, is merely Gombrowicz's ploy. He endows his narrator with his own name and his own real-life experiences only to surprise us with the jarring incongruity between the narrator's identity and the speech he uses consistently in his narrative monologue. The modern Polish writer is telling us, his modern readers, what happened to him after his arrival in Buenos Aires aboard a modern transatlantic liner, but he is doing so in the gawęda style of an old Polish nobleman: the only reaction can be a burst of laughter.

This is precisely the reaction *Trans-Atlantyk* was designed to provoke. After all, the grand finale of the novel is a gigantic burst of laughter. As Gombrowicz put it years later in his book of conversations with Dominique de Roux (published in English as *A Kind of Testament*), it was the grim hopelessness of Poland's mid-century ordeal under Hitler and Stalin that spurred him to seek a way out of the perennial Polish dilemma by imploding with laughter the very Form of being a Pole, the stereotype of "Polishness" as a mixture of martyrdom and empty gesture, a vicious circle of calls for compassion and pretenses of grandeur. His usual attitude of distancing himself from the Form has not changed at all in *Trans-Atlantyk;* rather, it focuses more specifically on "the national Form" in order "to wrest the Pole from Poland, so that he may become just a human being."

In 1953 this undertaking put Gombrowicz smack in the middle of a veritable minefield of national complexes and neuroses. It is to the eternal credit of the émigré publisher Jerzy Giedroyc and his Institut Littéraire that the novel came out then at all. Even the authority of the popular poet and novelist Józef Wittlin (himself an exile in New York), who wrote a preface for the book's first edition, could not save *Trans-Atlantyk* from the émigré public's outrage. The critics' responses ranged from contemptuous dismissals to uncontrolled fury. One of the most intriguing ironies of post-1945 Polish literature has been, however, the enormous difference between the rather predictable reaction of the émigré community (after all, for an exile, laughing at stereotypes of "Polishness" is more often than not tantamount to ridiculing the very value system that helps him overcome isolation among his host society) and the reception of *Trans-Atlantyk* in Poland itself. The political "thaw" of 1956 brought about the publication of several of Gombrowicz's books in Poland, by state-owned publishing houses and with the censor's official though short-lived blessing. *Trans-Atlantyk* appeared in 1957 and immediately became a modern classic, in spite of the modest printing of ten thousand copies. (Like the 1953 Paris edition, it was paired with the drama *Ślub* [The marriage].) It would be an exaggeration to say that its popularity spread beyond the cultural elite of Poland at that time; its impact, however, was lasting, especially among the young people who were its most ardent admirers. It was the novel's profound, Rabelaisian hilarity, its masterful way of bursting the bubbles of pomposity by inflating them beyond the limits of endurance, its irreverence toward grand words and sacrosanct myths, that gave many of us the mental fortitude to resist the totalitarian temptation, whether of the nationalistic or the communist variety.

One personal reminiscence involving *Trans-Atlantyk* will probably stick in my mind as long as I live. Faced with the nauseating prospect of taking the final exam in the course on Marxist political economy that all university students were then required to take, five friends of mine, Polish literature majors like myself, late one evening in May 1967 squeezed into my tiny room in downtown Poznań, purportedly to spend the night collectively cramming. None of us had opened the textbook before, although the examination was scheduled for the next morning. One of my guests vented his feelings: "OK, guys, it's obvious that the only thing we need to know for the exam is that Karl Marx was right, but we still could use some vocabulary to say it in at least a dozen different ways. What do you think? Can we manage this *and* still get an hour of sleep?" To relieve the tension, I answered by quoting my favorite line from *Trans-Atlantyk:* "I'm not so mad as to have any views These Days or not to have them." The roar of laughter that ensued convinced us that before we got down to serious work, we needed a couple of minutes of entertainment to clear our minds and lift our spirits. I reached for my dog-eared copy of Gombrowicz and read aloud the first two paragraphs. We took turns until dawn, one of us reading and the other five laughing ourselves to exhaustion, while our textbooks of Marxist political economy lay forgotten on the floor, never to be opened by any of us again.

Naturally, we all passed the exam that morning.

Stanislaw Baranczak

Translators' Note

In 1977, when we first considered our approach to *Trans-Atlantyk*, it soon became clear that we would not produce a conventional translation. The aim of literary translation is to make a foreign-language work into one of our own. But if we had tried to turn *Trans-Atlantyk* into either a modern English historical novel with archaisms (Barth, Burgess) or a period novel (Sterne), we would have lost more than we gained: namely, the Polish essence of the work, embodied in its unique style. *Trans-Atlantyk* is simply too Polish to be Englished, at least for the general reader. Moreover, to impose any literary form on this piece would be contrary to the central tenet of Gombrowicz's aesthetic.

Certainly with the publication of *Trans-Atlantyk* Gombrowicz proclaimed himself an intellectual maverick indifferent to readership. In *A Kind of Testament* he writes:

> *Trans-Atlantyk* was such folly, from every point of view! To think that I wrote something like that, just when I was isolated on the American continent, without a penny, deserted by God and men! In my position it was important to write something quickly which could be trans-

> lated and published in foreign languages. Or, if I wanted to write something for Poles, something which didn't injure their national pride. And I dared—the very height of irresponsibility!—to fabricate a novel which was inaccessible to foreigners because of its linguistic difficulties and which was a deliberate provocation of the Polish émigrés, the only readership on which I could rely!

Indeed, *Trans-Atlantyk* contained something to offend everyone. Not only did it baffle would-be translators, but it was hard to read in Polish. Many a Polish admirer of Gombrowicz today confesses not to have read it. What is more, it didn't seem to take itself seriously. With the war on and Poland in real danger, Gombrowicz should, he says, have written "something serious." But when he sat down to write:. "Instead of something serious—laughter, idiocies, somersaults, fun!" In fact, he acknowledges that "it was precisely this playful quality in *Trans-Atlantyk* which constituted its greatest provocation."

With this frank confession before us, how could we follow the example of the faithful but solemn German translation, or of the charming but inconsequential French adaptation (from which we borrowed *Filistria*)? If Gombrowicz would take such risks to maintain the integrity of his vision, how could we do less? What we had to do was to discover a very elastic style (or nonstyle) comprehending the archaic language, skewed and fragmented syntax, and unruly spirit of the original Polish that would be intelligible, even enjoyable, in English. Here was a superbly original mind at play in the field of language. We simply had to "let him out, give him free rein, let him frisk," and go with him wherever he led us—not only into incomparable imaginative flights, but into tortured syntax, ubiquitous repetition, anachronisms, inconsistencies, crude expressions, nonsense. Then our style would come.

We evolved a method of working together. Carolyn French, who did not know Polish, brought to the translation her scholar's knowledge of English literature, especially the literature of the seventeenth century, and her awareness of the flexibility of the English language. We worked together on the novel, discussing (often at length) each word in all its nuances, each structure, often reading aloud our English passages to test for sound. We consulted a great many texts, but the unabridged *Oxford English Dictionary* was our primary reference book.

Our first decision was not to use nineteenth-century English, though the much admired German translation (at that time the only one available) was set linguistically in that period. Gombrowicz wanted to create a showcase for baroque Polish, which he considered a richer, more vital language than that of the modern age. At the same time he mocked with parody the grandiose, romantic, sentimental "literary" language of nineteenth-century writers because it was so unlike the ordinary speech of real people. The old Polish gawęda, a literary genre that imitates spoken narrative, was the ideal vehicle for his purpose, and it was our belief that the language of seventeenth- and eighteenth-century England would best translate the novel that resulted. In seventeenth-century England there was not yet a literary language apart from poetry; English prose authors wrote the way they spoke. In the diaries of Pepys and Evelyn, in Urquhart's great translation of Rabelais, as well as in the lesser prose works of the period—Aubrey's *Brief Lives* or Aphra Benn's plays, for example—refinement and vulgarity of expression coexist as they do in *Trans-Atlantyk.* The period was best for our translation not only because of its language, but because we could portray grotesque characters and events as distant from our own time and therefore a bit more credible. Of course, when Gombrowicz strays from his period, we stray too—and at times, of necessity, we stray alone.

Our choice of period had its drawbacks. Seventeenth-century Polish is much closer to modern Polish than is seventeenth-century English to modern English. For this reason we usually translate metaphors literally rather than attempting to translate the meaning, which in many cases would have no equivalent in the language of our period. Metaphors resonate beyond their idiomatic meanings at the time of conception and are, in a sense, timeless.

Some passages in *Trans-Atlantyk* are triumphs of sound over sense. It was important for us to preserve the musicality of the Polish original. We have tried to keep the repetitive rhythms, refrains, alliteration, and rhyme as well as the imagery that lifts the prose to poetic (or mock-poetic) heights. Insofar as possible we have adhered to the original punctuation and capitalization in order to preserve the sketchy, sometimes elliptical "shorthand" style of the gawęda. Archaic words are rendered in archaic spelling, as are a few nonarchaic words like *show* and *while*, to suggest that we are flirting with the antique style but not wed to it. The novel does not make easy reading; it was not intended to do so. We have made few compromises for ease of comprehension.

One of our major obstacles was the enormous difference in cultures to be bridged. The central father/son metaphor, for example, did not translate. Whether England or America, ours has always been the "motherland," and since 1939 the "fatherland" has been Nazi Germany. Worse, present-day associations would impart to "fatherland" and "sonland" a kind of Disneyland banality at which Gombrowicz would have shuddered. Better, we thought, to use Latin words, in keeping with the gawęda and much less offensive to the ear. As for the wealth of parody, another obstacle, we found that if we translated accurately, the resulting exaggerations would be funny even to one not acquainted with the writers being parodied. The "empty, empty" refrain could, in fact, be a send-up of T. S. Eliot's "The Hollow Men."

Gombrowicz's verbs presented problems. Our rich treasury of verbs is the staple of English literature, but *Trans-Atlantyk* gave us precious little chance to exploit it. Gombrowicz uses the same simple verbs (walk, drink, go, show) over and over again, not only as verbs but as nouns, adjectives, refrains. The sound is somewhat varied in Polish because all parts of speech are inflected, but even when repetition is done for rhythmic effect, we had to use every ploy to avoid monotony in English. More difficult to overcome were the abrupt changes in tense—from present to past and back to present in one sentence—quite natural in Polish, not so in English. Here we had to compromise by regulating these changes so as to preserve both the casual gawęda style and the English reader's sanity.

Finally, there were words that had no real English equivalents: *gówniarz* and *bajbak*. The first, a term of contempt implying childish inadequacy, we translated by inventing the word "chitshit" (with a dot for delicacy where Gombrowicz uses three) to lighten the common English epithet. *Bajbak* (pronounced BUY-bahk, derived from the Ukranian *bobak*, meaning idler, lazy fellow) is an obscure Polish word, probably chosen by Gombrowicz partly because its very obscurity allows it to suggest more than the literal meaning would imply. We could have translated it with an even more obscure English dialect word *bibach* (from the Orkney Islands by way of Byelorussia), but this would only have compounded the reader's difficulty and necessitated a lengthy footnote. We chose instead to leave the word in Polish.

So we worked awhile on a literal translation, and gradually the unique English style we wanted began to emerge. In it were echoes of Urquhart, Aubrey, and Pepys; of Hudibras, Gulliver, and Tristram Shandy. Not to mention Gertrude Stein and T. S. Eliot, because *Trans-Atlantyk* is essentially a novel of twentieth-century —almost postmodern—sensibility: Nietzschean, Pirandelloesque, ironic, grand and absurd, full of melody and sour notes, hyperbole and pratfalls; in short, to borrow a descriptive phrase from an annual avant-garde arts festival—serious fun.

Throughout our endeavor the guiding principle was never for the sake of consistency or cleverness to impose literary form. So, though in general we stay with the baroque and avoid the nineteenth century, translate a word the same way each time it appears, retain imagery and sound patterns, refrain from clichés unless the author uses one, keep the tone light—sometimes we have to sacrifice one of these principles to make the best translation. After all, a work written over some years is bound to have inconsistencies, changes in style and point of view. Our resolve was to take any risk to let Gombrowicz speak to the reader in his own voice, if not his own language.

We consider our translation experimental. We have devised it in order to bring *Trans-Atlantyk* to as many English-speaking readers as will bear with it, even like it. We hope that ours will not be the last translation of this unique and important work.

The following glosses of words that appear in the text may be helpful:

Bife — Steak (Spanish)

Bigos — Polish or Lithuanian stew, traditionally served at the end of a hunt. Used figuratively in the sense of "hodgepodge."

Conies — Rabbits. In England, from the Elizabethan period to the early nineteenth century, it had the secondary meaning of dupes in a confidence game.

Ctvs. — Abbreviated plural of centavo, hundredth part of a peso (Spanish)

Kulig — An old Polish custom whereby, during carnival, a party of ladies and gentlemen in sleighs proceeded from manor to manor, perhaps in pursuit of a curlew *(kulig)*.

Palant — A Polish outdoor game played with a small, hard ball and a bat. The narrator deliberately confuses it with the Basque sport *pelota*, which was popular in Argentina in the 1940s.

Subhastation — An auction compelled by law. From the Latin meaning "under the spear."

Note on Pronunciation

Polish names are given in their original spellings. The stress (indicated below by capital letters) is on the penultimate syllable. The Polish *Pan*, *Pani*, and *Panna* correspond to the English Mr., Mrs., and Miss.

Bajbak	BY-back
Bumcik	BOOM-cheek
Cieciszowski	che-chee-SHOF-ski
Ciumkała	choom-KAH-wah
Doktorowa	dock-toh-ROH-vah
Dowalewiczowa	doh-vah-leh-vee-CHO-vah
Fichcik	FEEKH-cheek
Franciszek	fran-CHEE-sheck
Witold Gombrowicz	VEE-told gom-BROH-veetch
Grzegorz	GZHE-gosh
Henryk	HEN-rick
Ignacy	ee-GNAH-tzi
Ignasio	ee-GHAH-shoh
Józef	YOU-zef
Kaczeski	kah-CHESS-key

Kaliściewicz	kah-leesh-CHE-veetch
Kasper	CASS-per
Kiełbszowa	kyelp-SHOH-vah
Klejnowa	clay-NOH-vah
Tomasz Kobrzycki	TOH-mash cob-ZHITS-key
Konstanty	con-STAN-ti
Feliks Kosiubidzki	FE-lix koh-shoe-BITS-key
Kotarzycki	coh-tah-ZHITS-key
Kownacka	kov-NATS-kah
Krzywnicki	kshiv-NEETS-key
Kulaski	coo-LAH-ski
Kupucha	coo-POOH-khah
Liposki	lee-POH-ski
Lubek	LOO-beck
Ludka	LOOT-ka
Małgosia	mao-GOH-shah
Mateusz	mah-TEH-oosh
Mazik	MAH-zheek
Mazurkiewicz	mah-zoor-KYEH-veetch
Mickiewicz	meets-KYEH-veetch
Muszka	MOOSH-kah
Myszka	MISH-kah
Pankracy	pan-KRAH-tsi
Pindzel	PINDS-ell
Podsrocki	pot-SROTS-key
Polaski	poh-LAH-ski
Popacki	poh-PATS-key
Pani Pścikowa	PAH-knee pshchi-KOH-vah
Pyckal	PITS-cal
Rembieliński	rem-byeh-LIN-ski
Rotfederowa	rot-feh-deh-ROH-vah
Czesław Straszewicz	CHESS-wahf strah-SHEH-veetch
Szymon	SHI-mon
Szymuski	shi-MOOSE-key
Panna Tolcia	PAH-nah TOLL-chah

Note on Pronunciation		
	Panna Tuśka	PAH-nah TOOSH-kah
	Worola	voh-ROH-lah
	Panna Zofia	PAH-nah ZOFF-yah
	Zosia	ZOH-shah

Trans-Atlantyk

I feel a need to relate here for Family, kin and friends of mine the beginning of these my adventures, now ten years old, in the Argentinian capital. Not that I ask anyone to have these old Noodles of mine, this Turnip (haply even raw), for in the Pewter bowl Thin, Wretched they are and, what is more, likewise Shaming, in the oil of my Sins, my Shames, these Groats of mine, heavy, Dark with this black kasha of mine—oh, better not to heave it to the Mouth save for eternal Curse, for my Humiliation, on the perennial track of my Life and up that hard, wearisome Mountain of mine.

The twenty-first of August 1939 I was making to land in Buenos Aires on the ship *Chrobry*. Exquisitely pleasurable the sail from Gdynia to Buenos Aires, and somewhat loathe was I to go ashore, for twenty days a man between Sky and water, nothing remembered, bathed in air, melted in wave, through-blown with wind. Czesław Straszewicz, my companion, shared a cabin with me, viz. the two of us—as Literati (God forgive) scarce fledged—for this first voyage of the new vessel had been invited; besides there were Rembieliński, the Senator, Mazurkiewicz, the Minister, and many other people whose acquaintance I made. Likewise two Misses, pretty, Shapely, Willing, with whom in my spare moments I twaddled and dallied, turned their Heads, and so, I repeat, between Sky and Water, Tranquilly on and on . . .

Whereupon when we had landed, I, along with Pan Czesław and Rembieliński, the Senator, in the town ourselves immersed, wholly in the dark as in a Horn for none of us had ever set his foot here. The tumult, dust and greyness of the ground jarred unpleasantly after that pure, salt rosary of waves we had been saying on the Water. Albeit having passed Retiro Plaza, where the tower built by the English stands, we came apace to Florida Street and there Luxurious shops, an extraordinary abundance of Goods, merchandise, and the flower of distingué society, Houses of fashion, exceeding big, *confiseries.* There Rembieliński, the Senator, was looking over purses and I saw a poster on which the word CARAVANAS was written, and say I to Pan Czesław on this bright and Tumultuous day as we were strolling along: "Oooh, Pan Czesław, markye, mark here Caravanas!"*

But anon we needs return to the ship where the Captain was to entertain the Chairmen and Plenipotentiaries of our Polonia here. A large batch of those Chairmen and Plenipotentiaries came, and I anon made enemies, viz. amidst so many new, unknown visages as in a Forest lost, in ranks and titles lost, people, matters and things confused—vodka now did drink, now did not drink, and walked as if groping about a Field. Likewise His Excellency Minister Kosiubidzki Feliks, our envoy in this country, was honouring the Reception with his presence and, holding a glass, some two hours stood and by so standing now this one, now that one most graciously honoured. In the maelstrom of declarations and discourse, in the lifeless glare of lamps, as through a Telescope I observed it all, and Foreignness, Novelty and Quiddity seeing everywhere, beset by vanity and greyness, my home, my Friends and Comrades I summoned up.

* *In Polish,* karawan = *hearse;* karawana = *caravan (a company of merchants or pilgrims traveling together). In Spanish,* caravanas = *mobile homes.*

Albeit no matter. Yet something is amiss. Since, lookye, some sort of a hash has been made there, and though empty as in a field at night, there beyond the Forest, beyond the Grange, horror and Hell on Earth, as if something about to happen; but everyone thought all that would wash away, viz. a Great Cloud may give forth a little rain, and 'tis as with a Wench who Wallows, Howls, Groans, with that great Belly, Black, oh, Monstrous as if a Dragon she were to bring forth, but is only gripped by colic; hence no more fear. But something is Amiss, and belike Amiss, oh Amiss. In those last days before the War Broke out I, with Pan Czesław, Rembieliński, the Senator, and Mazurkiewicz, the Minister, were at many Receptions: viz. by His Excellency the Ambassador Kosiubidzki and the Consul, and a certain Marchioness at the Alvear Hotel, and God only knows who and what and where and for what reason, and wherewith and why; but when we were leaving these receptions, in the streets the annoying clamour of newscriers "Polonia, Polonia" would catch our ears. Ergo now 'twas ever the more hard, ever the more tristful, and everyone's ears droop low, and everyone walks as if Afflicted, stuffed as much with Care as with Delicacies. Whereupon Czesław with a paper bursts into our cabin (as still aboard ship we lived): "The war must break out today, tomorrow—no Remedy! The Captain has ordered that tomorrow our ship is to set sail since, though we cannot make through to Poland now, we will haply to somewhere on England's, Scotland's coast." When he uttered this, we into each other's arms in Tears did fall and anon to our knees did fall, God's help invoking and ourselves unto the Lord tendering. And so kneeling say I to Czesław: "Sail, sail you with God."

Czesław to me: "How so, but you are sailing with us!" Whereupon say I (and purposely have not got up from my knees): "Sail you and harbour safely." Says he: "What say you? You are not sailing?" Say I: "I would sail to Poland; but wherefore me to England? Wherefore me to England or Scotland? Here I will stay!" Thus I speak mumbling (as the whole truth I could not say) and he gazes and gazes at me. Spake he, very sorrowful now: "You would not with us? You prefer to tarry here? Then get ye to our Legation,

Report yourself there so that you'll not a deserter or perchance something worse be proclaimed. Will you go to the Legation, will you?" I replied: "What think you? Verily I will. I know my duty as a Citizen, for me be not worried. And better not tell anyone; haply I'll change my Intention and sail with you." Only then did I get up from my knees as the worst was over now, and good Czesław, good but Sorrowful, still proffered me his cordial friendship (though as if some Secret were between us).

I was loathe to reveal the whole truth to this man, to this Fellow Countryman, or to other Fellow Countrymen, Kinsmen . . . as I would haply be burnt alive at the stake, pulled apart by horses or tongs, deprived of good fame and credit. But the greatest difficulty of mine was this, that staying on the ship I could not by any means leave it secretly. Hence it was that, keeping a stern watch on myself before others, in the flurry of it all, in the quiver of hearts, in the exclamation of Ardour and Ditties, in the quiet sighs of fear and care, I as if along with the others Shout or Sing or Run or Sigh . . . but when they are undoing the ropes, when the Ship rattling with people, black with people, Compatriots, is just about to push off, to sail away, I, with the man who has carried my two cases after me, descend the gangway and begin my quitting. Thus I Quit. And I am not looking back. Quitting I am, and know naught of what now may be behind me. Yet I proceed along a gravel Way, and now have come quite far. Only when well Quit I was did I stand and look back and there the Ship has pushed off and is lying on the water, heavy, Squat.

Then would I fain have fallen on my knees! Albeit I did not fall at all, just quietly began to Curse, Damn mightily but only to Myself: "Sail, sail, you Compatriots, to your People! Sail to that holy Nation of yours haply Cursed! Sail to that St. Monster Dark, dying for ages yet unable to die! Sail to your St. Freak, cursed by all Nature, ever being born and still Unborn! Sail, sail, so he will not suffer you to Live or Die but keep you for ever between Being and Non-being. Sail to your St. Slug that she may ever the more Enslime you." The ship turned aslant now and was moving off so this I likewise say: "Sail to that Madman, to that St. Bedlamite of yours—oh, haply Cursed—so that he may Torment, Torture you by those leaps and frenzies of his, drown you in blood, howl at you and by his Howling howl you out, by Torturing torture you, Children of yours, wives, to Death, to Agony—in agony himself, in the agonies of his Madness Madden you, O'ermadden you!" With this Curse, turning my back on the Ship, I entered the Town.

I had ninety-six dollars in all, the which could suffice at best for two months of the most modest living, so it behooved me to rack my brain anon as to what and how. I thought to go directly to Pan Cieciszowski, whom I had known since the old days because his mother, having been widowed, near Kielce with the Krzywnickis lived, two miles from Cousins of mine, the Szymuskis, to whom sometimes with my brother and sister-in-law I did go, primarily to shoot Ducks. So this Cieciszowski, having been here for a few years, could be of service to me with some counsel and aid. To him at once with my bundles I went, and luckily it happened that I found him at home. 'Twas haply the most curious man I had met in my life, viz. Lean, slight, from a Sickness he had caught in his childhood exceeding Pale; despite all politeness, smoothness, as a Hare in a furrow pricks his ears, catches scent, now hurry-scurry Cries, now Quietens. Upon seeing me he exclaimed: "Whom do I see here!" and hugs, invites me to be seated, puts stools and bids in what way he might serve.

The true and weighty, Blasphemous cause of my remaining I could not reveal to him as, being a Compatriot, he could give me away. So I say only this, viz. that seeing I am cut off from my country, with great Pain, grievance, I have resolved to stay here rather than sail to England or Scotland and be a wanderer. With equal caution he replies that certainly in this need of our Mother's the good heart of each Son wings unto her; but, says he: "No remedy! I understand your Sorrow, but you can't jump over the ocean, so I approve of your Resolution or disapprove and well you did to remain here, but perchance you did Not." This he says, and Twiddles his thumbs. Seeing then that his thumbs he so twiddles, twiddles, I thought, why do you twiddle so; belike I will twiddle at you; and thereupon Twiddle my thumbs at him and say at the same time:

"Is't your view?"

"I'm not so mad as to have any views These Days or not to have them. But now that you have tarried here, get ye anon to the Legation or do not get ye there and Report your presence there or do not Report, for if you Report your presence or you do not Report it, you may be in great trouble or you may not."

"Do you believe so?"

"I do believe so or I do not. Do whatever you opine (here he is twiddling his thumbs) or do not opine (and is twiddling his thumbs) as 'tis your affair (again is twiddling his thumbs) whether something Bad will not befall you or Will" (and is twiddling again).

Then I twiddle at him and say: "Is this your counsel?" He is twiddling, twiddling and suddenly springs at me: "Miserable Man, you'd do better to Die, be Lost, quiet, hush, but do not go to them 'cause if they stick to you they will not come unstuck! Take my Counsel, you had better to keep with Foreigners, with them, be lost amidst Foreigners, be Dissolved, but may God save you from the Legation and likewise from the Compatriots for they are Bad, Wicked, Hell-sent, they will only Bite you, bite you to bits!" Whereupon I say: "Think you so?" To this he exclaimed: "God forbid that you shun the Legation or Compatriots living here 'cause if you shun them, you they will Bite, you they will bite to bits!" He is twiddling his thumbs, twiddling, I am twiddling too, and from that twiddling my head is twiddly, but something needs must be done as the purse is empty, so these words I said: "Could I not perchance some employment get in order to survive at least the first months? . . . Where could I find something?" He embraced me: "Fret not, we will presently take counsel; with the Compatriots I will make you acquainted; they will help you or they will not! There is no want of our moneyed merchants, industrialists, financiers, and somehow wangle you in I will, wangle . . . or no . . . " And he is twiddling his thumbs.

Heads together: "Ergo," he says, "there are three here who have a Partnership in Horses and likewise in Dogs, proffering dividends, and they may help you or may not, may hire you perchance as a clerk or an assistant with the salary of one hundred or one hundred fifty Pesos, as they are the most worthy, the best or not the best people; and they are partnered in a joint Stock company, engaged in Subhastation or not engaged; but there's the knot: to catch each one separate and separately in Private to him talk for there is from the old Times much Venom, Quarrel, and one is so Loathsome to the other that each is Loathsome with the other and simply Loathes. But the Knot is that one never a step takes from the other. Ergo, I would introduce you to the Baron as he is a generous wight, magnanimous, and he will not refuse you his favour; but what on't if Pyckal curses you and in Fair Choler abuses you before the Baron, the Baron rebuffs you before Pyckal, becomes sullen, and in a Whim against you lights into Pyckal; and Ciumkała cozens you before the Baron and Pyckal, perchance Besmirches. Ergo, the knot is you to the Baron against Pyckal, to Pyckal against the Baron" (here he is twiddling his thumbs).

About this and that we spoke for some while and likewise recollected friends of the old days, but at length (and perchance 'twas two in the afternoon then) to the pension which he had recommended I with my parcels went and there a small chamber for four pesos a day took. A city as any other. Houses some very tall, others low. In narrow streets a crowd so big that one can hardly pass, and a multitude of vehicles. Roar, rattle, toot, bellow, air unbearably humid.

~

Those first days of mine in Argentina I shall ne'er forget. The next day when I wak'd in my closet there came through the wall the cry of an Old Man, groans and lamentations, and from his plaints this only "guerra, guerra, guerra" I understood. So newspapers in shrill voice announced the outbreak of war, but who could know aught for one says this, another that, and all will be washed away or will not, they are embattled or they are not, and so naught—yet Grey, Eerie as a field in rain.

The day was fair, serene. In the crowd lost, my Lostness I was enjoying and even to myself aloud I say: "Naught to the eel when the Crayfish takes a beating." And there they are taking a Beating! In front of the News offices large swarms of people. I happened into a cheap hostelry to take sup and a "Bife" had for thirty ctvs., but say I (and still to myself): "The Greenfinch is healthy when the Ram is fleeced." And there they are being fleeced! Later to the river I went and there empty, quiet, breeze whiffling and I say to myself: "So, the Linnet chirps whilst the Badger in a Trap strives nearly out of his skin." And there nearly out of their skins . . . and beyond the Grange, beyond the Pond, beyond the Forest, awesome Yelling, Bellowing, Battling, Murdering, asking for mercy, granting no Pardon, and the Devil knows what, and perchance not even the Devil!

So say I: "Why me to the Legation; I will not go to the Legation, and since the Jade was Lean, let it Die." And there they Die. Then say I: "By everything that belongs to me I swear, and my oath on't, I will not meddle for 'tis not my Affair and if they are to perish, let them perish," but my eyes fell on a tiny Insect that was climbing up a grass blade and I can see that this Insect in this Place and Time, at this very moment on that Shore, on that side of the Ocean, is likewise climbing and climbing, climbing and climbing, and then the most terrible fear overwhelmed me and methinks I had better go to the Legation, oh best to go, yes, I'll go. I'll go, Jesus Maria, I'll go, I'd better go . . . and I went.

The Legation occupied a stately edifice in one of the more distingué streets. Having reached this edifice, I stopped there, and methinks go or not go as why should I go to the Bishop if from the Faith I am a backslider, a heretic, blasphemer. And presently a most terrible Vainglory, a Pride of mine that from my childhood has directed me against this Church of mine! Since not for this my Mother gave birth to me, not for this my Mind, Sublimity, my Art and the incomparable flights of my Nature; not for this the penetrating Sight, proud Forehead, Thought acute, passionate, so that I would in this homely Church, Worse, Littler, serve at Mass, oh haply Worse, Shabbier, in a shabbier, paltrier Choir, stupefy myself with paltry, middling incense along with other homely Homefolk of mine! Oh no, no, not for this am I Gombrowicz to kneel before the Altar dark, murky, and haply even Mad (but that Beating), no, no, I will not go, who knows what they can do to me (but Firing), no, no, I fain would not go there, poor, paltry Affair (but Slaughtering, Slaughtering!). And in Slaughter, in blood, in Battle, I entered the edifice.

And there quiet and a big Stairway cushioned with carpet. At the entrance a porter bowed me in and up the stairway to the Secretary led me. On the first floor a large hall with columns, quite dusky, cool, and only through the windows' coloured panes bunches of rays burst in and on cornices, heavy stucco-work, and gildings perch. Out to me came Podsrocki, the Counsellor, in a dark blue black Suit, High Hat and gloves and, lightly raising his High Hat, half aloud the reason for my visit enquired. When I said that I would like to talk to His Excellency the Envoy, he asked: "To His Excellency the Envoy?" Then say I, "To His Excellency the Minister," and says he: "To the Minister, to Pan Minister himself you wish to speak?" When I say, indeed, with His Excellency the Envoy I would speak, in these words he answered, lowering his head towards his breast: "Are you saying, with the Envoy, with Pan Envoy himself?" So say I, indeed with Pan Minister, as I have an important matter; then says he: "Ah! Not the Counsellor, not the Attaché, not the Consul, but the Minister himself you wish to see? But wherefore? For what purpose? And whom do you know here? And who are you? Who are your friends? Whom do you visit?" In this manner he started to interrogate me and more and more keenly to Spring at me, spring, and at last he started Searching me and took some string out of my pocket. Suddenly the far door opened and His Excellency the Envoy looked out and, since I was already known to him, Beckoned to me: upon this beckoning the Counsellor, gushing with bows and wagging his Rump and flirting with his High Hat, led me into the office.

Minister Kosiubidzki Feliks was one of the strangest people I've come upon in my life. Lean-Plumpy, somewhat fatty, he had a nose likewise rather Lean-Plumpy, an eye vague, fingers Slim-Plumpy and belike a Leg Slim and plumpy or fatty, and that Baldpate of his as of Brass over which he combed his black-red hairs; he was wont to flash his eye and every now and then he flashes it. By his behaviour and bearing he displayed extraordinary respect for his high dignity and by his every movement upon himself bestowed honour, and likewise continuously, mightily honoured by his Selfness the one he was talking to, so that one spoke to him almost on one's Knees. Instantly then, having burst into tears, I threw myself down at his feet and kissed his hand; and my services, blood, fortune offering, begged him to make use of me and place me at his disposal in this holy moment, according to his holy will, his reckoning. Most kindly honouring me and himself by his holy listening, he blessed and flashed at me, then says: "I cannot give you more than 50 pesos (he took out his purse). I shan't give you more since more I have not. But if you fain would go to Rio de Janeiro and hold to the Legation there, then I'll pay your fare and even add something to be quit of your hold as I would have no Writers here: they just Milk you and Bark at you. So get ye to Rio de Janeiro, I counsel you well."

Ergo that Surprise, Astonishment of mine! Again I threw myself down at his feet and (thinking he misunderstood me) offered my person. Says he then: "Ah, well, well, here have 70 pesos and Milk me no more for I am not a cow."

I see that he is fobbing me off with Cashes, and not just cashes but Small Coins! At such an Insult to me the blood rushes to my head, but naught say I. Presently I do say: "I see that for you, Your Excellency, very small I must be since you, Your Excellency, thus fob me off with Small Coins and belike number me with Ten Thousand writers and I am not just a writer but Gombrowicz!"

He asked: "And which Gombrowicz?" Say I: "Gombrowicz, Gombrowicz." Flashes and says: "Well, if Gombrowicz, have 80 pesos here and come no more—the War and Pan Minister is busy." "The War," I say. He says: "The War." Say I: "The war." He to this: "The War." So I to him: "The War, the war." He took fright in earnest so that his cheeks went white, flashed his Eye: "What? Have you any tidings? Has anyone told you aught? Any news?" . . . but checked himself: hems, coughs, scratches behind his ear and gives me a Pat: "Naught, naught, be not worried, we will vanquish the enemy!" And he instantly cried more loudly: "We will vanquish the enemy!" Then he cried more loudly still: "We will vanquish the enemy! We will!" He rose and cried: "We Will! We Will!"

Hearing these exclamations of his and seeing that he rose from his armchair to make Celebrations, even Exhortations, I fell on my knees and, in this holy Celebration enjoining myself, I did cry: "We will vanquish! We will, we will!"

He drew a breath. Did flash his eye. Did say: "We will, by my troth. I say this to you, and I say this so you cannot say that I was saying that we would not Vanquish, since I say to you that we will Vanquish, will Win, for we will reduce to dust with our mighty, gracious hand—smash, crush to dust, powder, with Sabres, Lances anatomize, annihilate, and under our Colours and in our Majesty, oh Jesus Maria, oh Jesus, oh Jesus . . . we will grind, Kill! Oh, we will kill, anatomize, demolish! And why are you staring so? I tell you indeed, we will annihilate! Indeed you can see, you can hear the Minister himself, the Gracious Envoy is telling you we will Annihilate; perchance you can see that the Envoy himself, the Minister, is pacing here before you, waving his hands and telling you that we will Annihilate! And don't you dare bark thus: that I didn't Pace before you, that I didn't Say, as you see that I do Pace and Say!"

Here he became surprised, gave me an Ox-Eyed glance and said:

"And 'tis I who before you Pace, Speak!"

Then he said:

"And 'tis the Envoy himself, the Minister who before you Paces, Speaks . . . So you can't be just a Cipher if His Excellency the Envoy himself is sitting with you for such a long time and is also Pacing before you, Speaking, even exclaiming . . . Sit you down, sit you down. And how do I call you, pray?"

"Gombrowicz," I say. Says he: "Oh yes, yes, I've heard, I've heard . . . How could I not have heard if I am Pacing before you, Speaking . . . One should come to your aid somewhat, Your Honour, since I am aware of my duty towards our National Literature and as Minister needs must come to your aid. Ergo, as you are an author, I could have you write for the papers here some articles, the which would praise, glorify our Great Authors and Geniuses; and for this, to beat a Krakowian bargain, I'll pay you 75 pesos a month . . . as more I cannot. A tailor cuts to the cloth. A dam is fitted to the pond! You can praise Copernicus, Chopin or Mickiewicz . . . Fear God, we have to praise Our Own else we will be swallowed!" Cheered, "Well said," he says, "and 'tis most Appropriate for me as Minister and likewise for you as Author."

But say I: "God reward thee . . . nay, nay." He asks: "How nay? Thou wouldst fain not praise?" Quoth I: "I am full of Shame." He cries: "How art thou full of shame?" Quoth I: "Shame, as our own!" Flash, flash, flash! "Why are you ashamed, sh.t!" he yells. "If we do not praise Our Own, who will?"

He drew a breath and said: "Know you not that every foxe praises his own tail?"

Said I, "I beseech your grace, Your Excellency, but I am exceeding full of shame."

Says he: "Have you Be-assed yourself, turned utterly Stupid, do you not see there's War and now, in this moment, Great Men are needed post-haste as without them the Devil knows what may happen, and I am Minister so as to add to the Greatness of our Nation. Oh, what am I to do with you, I will haply dust your Muzzle . . . " But he broke off, Flashed again, and says: "Wait. So you are a Writer? What have you scribbled? Books?" He called out

"Podsrocki, Podsrocki, come in here," and when Counsellor Podsrocki hurried in, he flashed at him and then talks with him and Flashes at me. I hear only that they say: "Chitsh.t." And again: "Chitsh.t." Whereupon the Counsellor says to the Minister: "Chitsh.t." Minister to Counsellor: "He certainly must be a chitsh.t, but the Eye, the nose good!" Says the Counsellor: "The Eye, the nose fair, although he is a Chitsh.t, and the forehead good too!" Says the Minister: "Chitsh.t and naught else for all of you are chitsh.ts. I am a Chitsh.t too, Chitsh.t, but Chitsh.ts they are likewise, and who will Perceive, who knows aught, nobody knows aught . . . who can understand aught, sh.t, sh.t."

"Sh.t," says the Counsellor. "Let him come out!" says the Minister. "I will Pace a bit and then Wham." And I see he has begun to Pace and is Pacing, Pacing around the salon, frowning, stooping, snuffling, soughing, swaggering, until he Hooted and Flashed: " 'Tis an honour for us! An honour since we are hosts to the Great Polish Author, perchance the Greatest! A great Author of ours, perchance even a Genius! Why are you gaping, Podsrocki? Greet the great Sh . . . that is . . . eh . . . Shining Genius of ours!"

Here the Counsellor makes a low bow to me!

Here His Excellency the Minister bows to me.

Here, seeing that they are scoffing at me, celebrating their joke, in my sore abuse I would fain beat this man! But an armchair the Minister is offering me! My boot Podsrocki, the Counsellor, is licking! My health the Minister-Envoy himself is asking, but at a 36-dollar black felt Hat is looking. His services the Counsellor is proffering! Now my desires and demands His Excellency the Envoy is enquiring! Now my inscription in the Visitors' Book the Counsellor is beseeching! Now my arm the Minister is taking to lead me around the salon, and the Counsellor is hopping around me, flitting to and fro! And the Minister: " 'Tis a feast day—Gombrowicz our guest!" And Podsrocki, the Counsellor: "Gombrowicz is a guest of ours, the Genius Gombrowicz himself." The Minister: "Genius of that Glorious Nation of ours!" Podsrocki: "Great Man of that great Nation of ours!"

So 'tis a strange, the strangest Event for me and Affair of mine! As I wit indeed that they are chitsh.ts who deem me a chitsh.t and all this is sh.t, sh.t, and fain would I knock the Noddles of those chitsh.ts . . . Albeit, indeed that's no one else but the Envoy himself, the Minister, and likewise the Counsellor . . . and from this that Shyness of mine, timorousness of mine when such important Personages make obeisance and do honour to me. And whilst in this Salon the Minister along with the Counsellor is flitting around me, Honouring me, whilst they are scurrying behind me, I, knowing the high Office, dignity, weight of these Chitsh.ts, could not free myself, flee all those honours! Like a plum in dung!

Thereupon the Envoy drew a breath and said, and more benevolently now: "But remember, you chitsh.t, that you have been properly honoured by the Legation, and now take care not to bring shame upon us with the people as we will shew you forth to People, Foreigners, as Great Sh.t Genius Gombrowicz. Propaganda requires this and it should be known that our Nation has geniuses in abundance. Will we not shew this, huh, Podsrocki?" "We'll shew it," said the Counsellor. "We will. Chitsh.ts they are and naught will they perceive!"

Only in the street did I give vent to my churned up feelings! Oh what, how, whence, what has happened?! Oh, it seems that I am caught again, caught! Oh Jesus, oh God, again I am caught up in my Life as a foxe in a snare! Never then will I liberate myself from my Lot? Must I repeat again that Eternal Lot of mine and Prison of mine?! And when my Past tosses me to and fro as a straw, when bygone Maelstroms resurge, I like a horse am straining, like a lion am rippling, Roaring, in fury with my paws am beating, with my whole self beating against the bars of a new prison! Oh, why did I go to that damned Legation?! So the chitsh.ts take a fancy to Greatness. They need Greatness, Geniuses, great Heroes to shew forth before People and belike we have that Genius Gombrowicz, hence how significant we are, what glory 'tis for us, and what merit, what a Palace of ours, what furnishings, harnesses, grandeur and tinsel; so

Fear God and let not our buttocks be beaten as that Genius Gombrowicz we have!

With this churlish turn His Excellency the Envoy sh.t sh.t would lather the eyes of the people, Foreigners, thinking rightly that he could easily convince those Americans, and if he bows low to me he will have me rise before the People like pastry. It cannot be so! Naught of this! And in that most terrible rage of mine over and over I dismissed, drove out, out with a cudgel, a club, out that Minister sh.t sh.t sh.t, out! Be damned the Minister sh.t who has no respect for his Nation! Be damned the nation that has no respect for its Sons! Be damned the man and Nation that have no respect for themselves! And I, distraught, the Minister, offices all, honours, titles, times of ours, life of ours, Nation, Country sh.t sh.t sh.t dissipating, devastating, with a club, a cudgel hurtling, again that paid Minister chitsh.t dismissed; and when some 50 or 60 times I had dismissed him, dissipated him, I kept dismissing him and dispensing with him over and over again! But then I noticed that I was causing laughter amongst the passers-by who gave me looks.

The pressing state of my Finances compelled me to act; and presently I must go to Florida Street where I am to meet Cieciszowski. Florida Street, as I have already mentioned, of all streets of the city the most luxurious; shops there, comely Establishments of all kinds there, cafés, confiseries there; vehicles forbidden there, flocks of strollers there; with sun made bright, it sparkles, shimmers, swaggers with a peacock's tail.

My inborn shyness and perchance some Embarrassment as well did not allow me to give Cieciszowski a more detailed report of what had happened with the Minister, so I mentioned only that we had parted in anger. "Oh!" he exclaimed, twiddling his thumbs. "Why did you go there; I told you not to go there, but perchance you did well to Go there! 'Tis good you wiped his nose, or perchance 'tis Not good, since, oh, now he will yours, Woebegone, wipe, wipe, wipe! Hide yourself, hide in a mousehole, since if you do not hide yourself they will find you! But do not hide yourself, do not hide, I say, for if you hide they will seek you out, and if they seek you out they will find you . . . " But we, in conversation, are strolling along Florida Street! There behind the vitrines the wealth glitters, lures the eye, hummy buzz, passers-by, bowing and greeting.

Now and again that Cieciszowski of mine sends out to acquaintances a smile or a gesture or a low bow and says to me quietly: "Lookye, lookye—can you see Pani Rotfederowa? This is Director Pindzel, and this Chairman Kotarzycki. Hey, Chairman—Hola! Hola! This is Mazik, and this one Bumcik, this is Kulaski, and that one Polaski!" Beside him I likewise bow politely, cast smiles right and left, and Florida's snake shimmers, Señoritas on parade!

"Lookye, Pani Klejnowa stands there! And that is Lubek, a clerk." But thicker the swarm of people and they stop at *vitrines*, regard them, and when from one go, instantly to another go, and then one at Ties, yellow-grey, fashionable at 5.75 dollars, and Another with his Wife at a carpet, wine-red, Mottled, for 350, and a fourth at English Buckles at 99, a fifth at gadgets or a fan; she there at lingerie silk, frothy, she here at Shoes à la Nelson, pointed, with double soles, that one at a Pipe Tobacco Persian-Astrakhan, or a dinner Service, or else Cinnamon. At a valise, Yellow, chamois, for 320 they look and say: "What a valise!" But likewise a Bucket for 85—not bad either, or this Dressing Gown or that Shovel. "I would buy this sombrero for 7.20.—And I this 'sweater.'—I could use that Thermometer or that Barometer.—Mercy, this umbrella with the bent handle costs 42 dollars and yesterday I saw a better one, English, for 38!" And so from shop to shop, at this and that Stared and Compared, and then again to another Shop and again Comparing and Staring.

Suddenly Cieciszowski seized my hand. "You were born with a cawl! Can you see the Baron? The Baron stands there; you have caught the Baron himself; he is at a vitrine and on his own, without his Partners. Let's go to him or not go to him; we'll talk to him about your work or we will not! Let me greet you, dear Baron, how's your health, how do you fare or Not fare? This is Pan Gombrowicz who, by consequence of being cut off from the Country, has remained here and with us lives through our uncertitude and fear, and likewise seeks some employment!" The Baron looked at me and most cordially seized me in his arms! Then, joyful, he springs back and springs forth again, hugs me to his breast, "Perchance we might have a nibble or a nip," invites me to his home and is looking for his Wife who got lost somewhere as to his Wife he wishes to introduce me. "Stop with us on Tuesday! We shall be pleased!" But Cieciszowski said: "He could do with an occupation for he is in need, and as swiftly as smoke I him to you, gracious Baron! Lavish set, lavish food."—"Psht!" exclaimed the Baron. "Need? 'Tis already settled! Trouble yourself no more! Anon today I'll order that you be appointed by the Partnership as my secretary with a salary of 1000 or 1500 pesos! Psht! Settled! The working hours you will choose yourself! So 'tis settled and now a Nip on't—a nibble is what we need!"

So we are going with the Baron to have one, and in the glare of sun everything seems to be cast in order and I a Protector, Father and King magnanimous haply have found. Oh, thank you, God, and now 'twill be easier for me to live, cares and sorrows are bygone and vanished—but what is't? God, oh God of mine, what goes here? Why has the King, this Baron of mine, subsided, quietened and now turned sullen, wan; why is that sun of mine setting behind a cloud? . . . Ah, 'tis Pyckal; Pyckal springs on us!

Pyckal, the Baron's partner, was shorter than the Baron, stockier, and whereas the Baron was a magnificent, magnanimous, manly, noble Man, Pyckal was as if pulled from a dog's throat or from behind a barn. In vain the Baron gives him Orders and states he has appointed me, a friend of his, as clerk; in response Pyckal only bumped, first at me then at the Baron and, Spitting, said, "Didye get dumped on your head to take on new Clerks for the Office without consulting me?! Are ye a Cretin? So for you I will drive out that clerk of yours, out, out, out!" By such terrible boorishness shaken, the Baron at first could not utter a word, then "I forbid it!" he cried, "I disallow!" At which Pyckal disgorged at him: "Forbid yourself, not me! Who are you forbidding?!" Shouted the Baron: "Please make no scandals!" Cried Pyckal: "Delicatus, delicatus—I will Pound that delicatus of yours, I'll pound him Down!" . . . And towards me with his fists, and perchance he will Pound me, pound me out; belike he will pound me down, this beast, this bully, will butcher me, so Doom, Destruction for me, but what goes? Why does that Butcher of mine stay, why does he not pound on me? Ah, 'tis Ciumkała, the third partner of the Baron, from somewhere come forth!

Ciumkała, raw-boned, a blond, Oggling, ruddy, has taken off his cap and his Big Red hand puts out towards me: "Ciumkała I am." And by this he put Pyckal into sudden amazement. "Save me!" yelled Pyckal, "I am pounding this one here and he breaks in with his paw and I haven't seen with my own eyes a bigger Idiot, Blockhead. Why do you break in, why do you meddle?" "I forbid it," shouted the Baron, "I disallow!" Ciumkała, frightened by this shouting, became embarrassed and put a big Hand into his pocket and with that hand began to paw about within the pocket; but at once became embarrassed by his Pawing and out of his embarrassment pretended he was trying to find something in his pocket; and by this he made the Baron, Pyckal all the more furious. "What are you looking for, you numskull?" they cried. "What are you looking for, you daw? What? . . . " Till Ciumkała, well-nigh dead from embarrassment, as a Beetroot red, took out of his pocket not only his hand but also a cork, some crumpled scraps of paper, a teaspoon, a shoestring, and some small dried fishes. But when they saw the Fishes, silence set in . . . as they had turned somewhat downcast because of those Fishes.

I remembered what Cieciszowski had told me that amongst them there were, as amongst Partners, old Splinters, Venoms and Acids, apparently about a Mill, a Dyke; and indeed for this reason Pyckal, seeing those Fishes, gasped and "My crucians, my Crucians!" he yelled, "you'll Pay for them, I'll send you off a pauper." But the Baron only agitated his Adam's apple, gulped, adjusted his collar, and said: "The ledger." To this Ciumkała said: "The Barn got burned 'cause of that Buckwheat," whereupon Pyckal looked askance and muttered: "There was water." And so they stood, Stood until Ciumkała scratched himself behind the ear; and whilst he is scratching behind the ear, the Baron rubs his ankle and Pyckal his right shin.

Says the Baron: "Scratch yourself not." Says Pyckal: "I'm not Scratching myself." Ciumkała said: "I have Scratched myself." Said Pyckal: "I'll Scratch you." Says the Baron: "Scratch, scratch away—this is what you are for." Says Pyckal: "I'll not Scratch you, let your Secretary scratch you." Says the Baron: "My secretary will Scratch me if I order him to." Said Pyckal: "I will engage your Secretary for Myself and take him from you—and me he will Scratch when I would, for though you are a High-born Sir and I a Base-born Boor, me he will Scratch if I would so or would no. Scratch he will." Says the Baron: "Whether a Base-born boor or a High-born Sir, you will not engage this Secretary; I will engage him for me, and he will Scratch me, not you."

Cries Ciumkała then, in full, wistful plaint: "Oh, Help, help! All for yourself to yourself you would fain Scratch, at my Expense, with a Loss to me, Disaster; oh, then I'll him, not for you—for me engage, I'll him Engage!" Then they drag me, pull; one tugs me from the other, Drag, Drag, and so they dragged me to a house, there Steps, up these steps they drag, tug; one wrests me from another; there a small side door and on it a board: "The Baron, Ciumkała, Pyckal: Equine-Canine Trade." And beyond the door, a Hall large, darkish; in it Chairs. In a chair the Baron to Ciumkała, Ciumkała to the Baron, to Pyckal, Pyckal to Ciumkała, to the Baron had me seated and, having asked me most politely to wait awhile, they went to another room, on the door of which there was a sign: "Properties and Transactions Management, Entry Prohibited."

Left alone (for Cieciszowski long ago had made himself scarce) in the quietude that set in after that noisy entry of ours, I looked about with curiosity. The strangeness of these people (and in all my Life it would be hard to search out stranger ones) and the brawl they had been having amongst themselves greatly disinclined me from any contact with them; but hope for permanent and perchance higher wages compelled me to remain. The hall, as I say, was darkish, lined with dark wallpaper, but paper much frayed . . . or a grease Spot . . . or a Hole or a slight Rip, but mended, by flies bespeckled, and a candlestick with a candle, stearin splotched everywhere. Floorboards tattered, from walking worn, and there, in a Corner, an old newspaper; here a Whip babbles secretly whilst the Newspaper moves with a rustle as haply Mice are sitting under it. Presently likewise a Boot has begun to move and come nigh some Tobacco, and a small Insect that issued from a slit in the floor is industriously making for Sugar.

Amidst these rustlings I slightly opened the door that led to the next Room. A big room, long and Darkish, and a row of tables at which clerks sit, over Promissory Notes, Ledgers, Folios studiously bent; and such a number of Papers, so lumped, Swamped that you can hardly move, for likewise on the floor there a multitude of papers and old scribblings; and Ledgers from a cupboard protrude and even to the ceiling heave, out onto the windowsills bulge and swamp the whole Office. So if any of the clerks moves, he rustles as a Mouse in these papers. Albeit, amidst the papers, there are many other things as Flagons, or bent tin, further on a broken saucer, spoon, a shred of muffler, bald brush, further on a piece of brick, next a corkscrew, a scrap of bread, many Shoes, likewise cheese, feathers, Kettle and umbrella. Closest to me a Clerk, old, thin, sat and a nib under the light scrutinized, with his finger testing it, and as if he suffered from Gum-boil, some cotton wool in his ear; behind him another Clerk, younger and red-cheeked, on an abacus counted whilst chewing a sausage; further on a lady clerk with her hair cosseted, kiss-curled, is inspecting herself in a mirror and adjusting her curls; and further on other clerks, of the which perchance there were eight or ten. This one is writing; and that one is searching through a Ledger. Whereupon Tea was brought in, viz. Mugs with coffee and buns on a tray, and then all the clerks, having paused in their work, set upon the food. And anon, as usual, discourse sounded. I was overcome by laughter at the sight of that Coffee Drinking of those clerklets! Since at first sight one could see that, for years sitting together in this Office, every day the eternal Coffee drinking and the eternal Bun munching, with these same old jokes treating themselves, they at once all there was of theirs comprehended.

So the lady clerk pushed back her curls and said "Plunk" (she has haply said it some thousand times), to which the fat cashier who sat behind her exclaims thus: "Hi diddle diddle, Mother Squiddle!" from which an extraordinary Glee; all the Clerks are laughing, holding their tummies! But scarce had that laughter sunk into the Papers, when the old Accomptant wagged his finger . . . and all hold their tummies as they know what he is about to say . . . and he says: "Squiddle fiddle, de dum dum Diddle!" So the Clerklets, even more gleeful, in papers rustle. But the Lady Clerk her right cheek on the Little Finger of her left hand rested! But the Lady Clerk her cheek on her Little Finger rested! . . . And then the Accomptant rapped the shoulder of the red-cheeked Under-Clerk hard and whispers to him: "Waste no tears, no tears waste, Józef, Józef; for Penknife, saucer, fly, a Fly was there!" . . .

I could not understand why the Accomptant spoke to him of Tears if he was not crying . . . but in this very moment the red-cheeked Bookkeeper lapsed into suppressed sobbing at the sight of that Little Finger! So again I was seized by laughter: seemingly year upon year, and for ages that Little Finger, along with the Cheek, scratched old wounds of the bookkeeper the which festered in his heart, and perchance for years that companion of his had given him some consolation; but instead of the Bookkeeper crying first and the Accomptant then consoling him, the sequence of actions was confused by them and what had been the End went to the beginning! The Lady Clerk tossed up a handkerchief! The cashier gave a sneeze! And the old accomptant wiped his nose! Suddenly they noticed me and, becoming terribly embarrassed, into their papers as Mice caved.

But anon I was summoned to the Principals. A closet, darkish, where I was led likewise filled with papers, old scribblings;

and what is more, an old iron Bed stood by the wall and likewise a bucket, likewise a Wash Bowl, a double barrel on the window, shoes, Flypaper. Pyckal a crate for the Baron held whilst Ciumkała some receipts from a Ledger read. And All three to me: "Me, scratch me! Scratch me! Scratch me!"

~

In this whole life of mine many strange places and even stranger people have I beheld, but amidst those places and people naught so bizarre as this present episode of my Life. The inveterate quarrel between the Baron, Pyckal and Ciumkała had its beginning in a Mill, the which fell to them in equal parts from the Liquidation; then in three inns put out to lease it was rekindled yet the more strongly. And when a Still (with right of propination) was taken as the result of subhastation apparently to make payments, the more the strife, the venom. The division of funds was well-nigh impossible to execute since the court's judgment was appealed twice by each of the three parties, the judicial hearing six times adjourned; in the end, for the lack of written proof, a Survey was ordered, the which Survey shewing obvious contradiction between the first and second record of Subhastation. And to all this a mutual summoning for Usurpation of Property, threats and desire to murder, Kill, and two summonses for Foray and one for appropriation of six pearl pins and a Ring . . . and so summonses, forays, assaults, strifes, venoms, desire to Kill, deprive of Property, ruin, send off a Pauper. So when as Surety for Subhastation, the equine-canine Trade was to be taken over on the basis of the Record, all three of them acceded to this Trade in equal parts, and Dogs, Horses buying up from people, sold them at great profit. Albeit, although despite highly noteworthy profits from this Trade, the partnership was threatened by Bankruptcy since, lookye, so many old Furors, Assaults, so much mutual munching, crunching, so much bitterness, so many Acidities, and that Hell-mongering rabid, without end.

But this quarrelsomeness not so much perchance out of financial settlings as out of differings in natures. Since the Baron as a Bumblebee whirrs and soars and Bounces, as a Peacock swaggers his tail, as a Falcon flying on high; and Pyckal as a Bull with his bawling, howling churlish, churlish charges; and Ciumkała Paws about; and the Baron as if driven in a carriage, four horse, Orders gives and a Trumpet trumpets; and Pyckal stuffed with churlishness just Gawps it out; and Ciumkała with Cap in fist for that ensliming of his; so the Baron Whims, Moods, Caprices, Fancies; so Pyckal would a muzzle slap or his Breeches shed; so Ciumkała licking or Dawdling . . . Ergo one would drown the other in a spoon of water, but in the continuous sequence of Trials, summonses, quarrels, in that ceaseless Gnawing communion, so one with the other as bigos, as Hodgepodge mixed, stewed, that perchance one cannot live without the other and in this mouldy Cheese, in this inveterate Boot of theirs, as Toes bent, Hideous, and with themselves only! Ergo they are with themselves! Ergo they are amongst themselves! And they have forgotten God's world, with themselves only, amongst themselves, self-selved; and from the old days so many Relicks have piled up, so many reminiscences, rancours, divers words, corks, old Flagons, Double-Barrels, tins, divers rags, bones, brads, saucepans, scraps of tin, ringlets, so that no stranger who approached them could sense what they to him will say or do 'cause a Cork or a Flagon or a word heedlessly thrown out at once reminds them of something Older and Baked In, and moves them as a weathercock on a Church tower.

Ergo, if not for the old Fishes that had then fallen out of Ciumkała's pocket, if not for the Ledger, and scratching the Leg, I perchance would not have been engaged as a clerk by them. But alike for the reason of a small Flagon or a Crate, instead of 1000 or 1500 Pesos that had been promised by the Baron as my recompense, only 185 Pesos I was given. And also the oldest Clerks, when they went to the Principals with their deeds, documents, never knew what, lookye, was going to be fried up for them, what decision Pyckal to the Baron, the Baron to Ciumkała, Ciumkała to the Baron, to Pyckal would give. Ergo, many commands, orders, many affairs: now Horses ceded, now a mortgage transferred, next surety, sharing of dividends, Dogs pawned (Bulldogs only), propination, execution; so documents they write, scribble; Accompts, summonses issue, enforce; bid, further mortgage or Subhastate; but, lookye, what matter if behind all that, under it, an Old herring or a Bun which the Baron nipped from Pyckal seventeen years ago.

When next morning I presented myself at work and amidst the Clerks, now Colleagues, sat, the difficulty of this new duty of mine appeared to me clearly. The clerks, deep in their Papers, to their Accompts devoted, in their functions, duties anxious not even to look at me, a stranger; yet to me their Crabbings, their old jars, were incomprehensible and unfathomable.

Popacki, the old Accomptant, gave me Deeds to enter, but the devil knows whether there was any need for that entering, viz. that man, not large in stature, very Thin, in glasses dark, horn-rimmed, as a mummy dried up, with Sparse hair that as a wreath wrapped around his large Bald pate; and also Fingers long, lean. Watching my work, this or that character he corrects for me now and again, and scratches himself behind the ear, or wipes his nose, or flicks a mote off his suit; but most eagerly breadcrumbs for sparrows through the window throws. Ah, plainly a good soul the Accomptant, good soul to the bone, and although this plodding of his and extraordinary punctiliousness in everything frequently made me laugh, I avoided everything that might hurt the dear old man; and would even take his snuff, the which, long since hatched in some mouse's nest, and who knows by what Mould seasoned, of his Cashmere waistcoat smelled.

But, in sooth, I was not disposed to laugh. Although my existence being somewhat secured, the complex of all conditions and circumstances as: viz. a Country Foreign, the strangeness of the city, want of friends or confidants, oddness of that Work of mine . . . filled me with some fear; to this also heavy Combat beyond the water and with bloodshed, and many people, friends of mine or relations, now no one knows where are, what do, perchance give souls to God. Thus although far away, beyond the water it was, one is somewhat more Careful, more quietly speaks, more calmly Moves so as not to arouse an Evil, and as a Hare would crouch in a furrow. Therefore a small Crumb of bread on an inkpot having noticed, I often upon this crumb did look and it even with the end of my pen did touch . . .

Yet my affair with the Legation galled me most of all. But surely His Excellency the Envoy had not celebrated his Celebrations with me to let them be washed away; and when I sit at the desk, Deeds enter, they perchance theirs, and who knows if they are not, though without my knowledge, doing something further with me. So sit I, write, but think what are they with me, what do they take of me, make of me. Indeed, my presentiments did not deceive me for when in the evening I returned to the Pension, a large bouquet of white and red fuchsias from the Minister was handed me, and with it a letter from the Counsellor. In the most polite words the Counsellor advised me that on the morrow he would call to take me to the painter Ficinati's for the soirée, the which was to be honoured by the presence of Writers and Artists from hereabouts. Besides this letter and the flowers, two more Bouquets were handed me, the which came from our native Chairmen from hereabouts, and both with ribbons and appropriate inscriptions. Further besides, little Children arrived, and at my window Canticles sang.

The Devil take it! When I am for crouching, they would light me high with candelabra! Astounded by the abundance of homages, the proprietress of my Pension would not hear of my staying any longer in that tiny cell of mine and to the best chamber transferred me: so, in these difficult, dangerous times of mine, instead of in a little chamber, in a large Salon with two windows I did find myself. By now the news about that surpassing, God forgive, eminence, greatness of mine went swift as darts amongst all Compatriots: the next day in the Office with very low bows I was received and well-nigh all discourses, raillery in my presence were abandoned.

The Devil with it, the Devil! Mightier and mightier the Celebration was becoming and seemingly His Excellency the Envoy against my will and with no heed to my violent aversion did as he would, and was spreading the Celebration in divers parts. A pox on't, whyever did I shew myself before his eyes! And 'tis dangerous, moreover! In normal times such trumperies may be performed, but when over there Slaying, Slaughtering, 'tis better to sit quietly and attend, and take care so as not to call down some evil on oneself.

I kept swearing and resolving that I would not go to that Reception and any further St. Celebration—oh, Silly mayhap, Paltry—of my person I would not permit. Albeit the Knot is: viz. if now I were to resist the plain desire of His Excellency the Envoy, perchance by all I would be taken as a traitor, the which in the present set of circumstances would exceeding dangerous be. But indeed, sweet the homage of compatriots to a man who since the earliest days of his childhood contempt only has experienced . . . when here as if by a good fairy they begin to lower their heads before him and take Hat in hand before him. Cursed then, false the homage and likewise exceeding paltry! Yet holy, blessed, true homage as that Forehead of mine, that Eye of mine, that Thought of mine, that truth of mine, and the sincerity of that heart of mine, and that song of mine, and that dignity of Mine! Ergo, this is my right, this is my ermine, this is my crown! And why look a gift horse in the mouth! Oh, so haply I shall go to this Assemblage and permit them to do all that with me there, as I swear by God and my Mother before God, Altar, that he who comes to me with hat in hand does naught wrong, indeed, he does what is best, most right!

So you there, chitsh.ts, Wile, Guile, and for your own profit as fowls peck. Whatever conceived by your Nature, blunt and wily, I will take according to my Nature and whilst with sh.t you feed me, I as Bread and Wine will eat it and will be Filled. Yet when I as a true master at that reception shine, when as a Master by foreigners am recognized, acclaimed, then His Excellency the Envoy's folly will dismay me no more, and he needs must respect me, too . . . Then mount, mount that Horse they are readying for you, and you will go far! Therefore attend I will, I will!

Whereupon, having returned to my Pension, I opened my trunk at once, and shaving myself, changing, donning my attire, I felt the extraordinary certainty of my Masterdom, and I knew that I had to predominate, dominate all of them. Oh Master, Master, Master and Master! But amazement and Astonishment of mine! For suddenly this utterance behind me I heard: "Hail to our great Author, hail to the Master!" I flinched and cried out, thinking that was the utterance of a scoffer or perchance that it even came out of me. And here Podsrocki, the Counsellor, in striped trousers and tailcoat, all à la pug under hat, is bowing down to me: "Your Excellency, Sir! By request of His Excellency the Envoy I have come here in a cabriolet. Shall we go then?"

The sound of that plain lie, abruptly before me embodied, was as a whack in the mug! Oh, wherefore does this chitsh.t who thinks me a chitsh.t call me Master? Now we get into the Cabriolet. Now in the cabriolet we are riding; and though heavily bestowing honours, homages each on the other, yet knowing that he knows that I know that he knows that I know, and sh.t, sh.t, sh.t, heavily contemning each other we are; and so in honours and in sh.t we draw up before the house.

And there, scarce had I alighted from the cabriolet, straightway at me that batch of Compatriots and "Hail, hail," "Be welcome, be Welcome," and "glory, fame"; now flowers proffer, now make merry as if 'twere Christmas; and amidst them the Baron; also Pyckal; next Cieciszowski, and also Ciumkała and the Cashier, and the Bookkeeper, and Panna Zofia in a yellow damask gown. In sooth they honour me! The Counsellor beside me most politely to the right, to the left bows; I also bow, greet and so amidst Honours we proceed into that house. And there Quiet.

I found myself in a large salon; and there many people, some standing and some sitting; and all that eating of petits fours, sipping of wine with Glasses, Goblets in hand; now there a Woman holding out her hand for a Glass; somewhere else a threesome or foursome a book or a Bottle inspects; there sitting in a circle they are, and talking. Yet not clatter or noise but unusual Quietude for, although there was no want of discourse and even laughter, discourse, laughter, exclamations instead of being a bit louder were indeed a bit softer, quietened, and that Motionlessness of motion as Fishes in a pond. The Counsellor politely bent in half, fanning with a handkerchief, leads me to the Host, to him introduces me, and as the Master Great Polish Genius Glorious Gombrowicz praises me. The host, plump, round, the Counsellor's fanfare with a low bow receives and knowing not how enough to Honour, in courtesies, flourishes melts away . . . but a Blond lady, thin, small, accosted him and he began to converse with her, forgetting us. Ergo we stand. But to an Old, thin, grey-haired man who was perchance a distinguished guest, the Counsellor leads me and with a fanfare introduces me elaborately—so that the Old Man Bows and honours as one can . . . but what, since he Forgets us anon as his shoelace has become untied. So we to the third, who of a seemly height, grizzled, and this one clasped his head: "Such an honour!" exclaims . . . but he took a petit four, ate it, and forgot. Thus, with the Counsellor in the middle we stand, say little, and behind us other Countrymen Kinsmen likewise stand and little say. Say little.

"Hold," said the Counsellor . . ., "we'll shew them." Ergo we stand, and about us other Guests stand, some hundred perchance. Very richly dressed and neat, as shirts of Silk or of Cambric for 13, 14 or even 15 Pesos, ties, Cravats, or modish Lorgnettes, likewise Pumps, then narrow-rimmed Heels, kerchiefs, lip rouges, ankle boots of English style for 20 or 30 Pesos. But primarily Men's socks struck the eye, and by pulling up their trouser legs, they these Socks eagerly shew, whilst ladies do each others' Hats assess. So one pats the other. One the other tenderly embraces: "Amigo, amigo"—"Que tal?"—"Que es de tu vida, que me cuentas?" But despite that tenderness, cordiality, now and then the Discourse subsides or falls off for one speaks and the other in distraction, in some Forgetfulness now has stopped listening, now is inspecting his Sock. So they are saying: "Is that Revista out yet?"—"I was paid 50 Pesos for an article"—"How are you, how are you! What news?"—"How much was that Land?"—"I acquired Socks for myself."

Then all together hands raised up and their heads clasping

cried aloud: "Oh, what do we Say? Oh, why can we not say our Say?! Oh, why do we not Respect and Honour each other?! Oh, why so Shallow, so Shallow?!" So one to the other Flits, one bestows Honour on the other, one to the other "Maestro, maestro" and "Gran Escritor" and "Que Obra" and "Que Gloria" but what, since it falls off anon and again in distraction they are inspecting Socks.

"Hold," said the Counsellor, "Hold . . . We will shew them yet!" Yet we stand. To me whispered the Counsellor, pale and sweaty: "Shew something, chitsh.t, to those chitsh.ts else we will be shamed!" Say I to him: "You chitsh.t, what am I to shew them?" And behind me My Own stand and seeing that no one takes any notice of me perchance think me a chitsh.t, angry as Sin, so angry they would drown me in a spoon of water! To the Devil, to the Devil, to the Devil! The Devil! Perchance something Amiss! But I see that new people are coming in, and not just any people for anon Bows, Honours wafted towards them.

So first entered a lady in an ermine Cape, with Ostrich, Peacock Plumes, and with a large Purse; beside her some Lickspittles and after the Lickspittles some Scribes, next some Scribblers and some Jesters who beat the Drums. Likewise amongst them a wight Clad in Black, and seemingly distinguished for when he entered voices could be heard: "Gran escritor, maestro"—"Maestro, maestro" . . . and out of this admiration they might have fallen on their Knees, save they were eating petits fours. Anon then a circle of listeners unfurled and he in the center began to make his mighty Celebration.

That man (and haply so strange a man for the first time in my life had I seen) was uncommonly pampered and, what is more, was still Pampering himself. In a Greatcoat, behind large Black glasses as if behind a fence from the whole World shut off, around his neck a silk scarf with demi-pearl grey dots on't, on his hands Demi-gloves of black cambric, on his head a hat, demi-brimmed, black. So muffled and apart, now and then he took a sip from a narrow flask, or with a Kerchief of black cambric mopped himself and fanned. In pockets Papers aplenty, scripts the which he ceaselessly mislaid, and under arm Books. Of intelligence enormously subtle the which he in himself all the time ensubtled, distilled, in every utterance of his so intelligently intelligent he was that the Women's and Men's delighted clucks arose (even though they inspect Socks, ties). That voice of his he quietened constantly but, the Quieter the louder indeed, as others, having quietened themselves, all the more intently did listen (though they Listen not); and so he in the Black Hat seemed to lead his brood into the Eternal Quietude. Looking into his books, notes, mislaying them, Wallowing, weltering in them, with rare quotations he sprinkled his thought and capered with it to and for Himself, as in a solitary. And so whimsically coddling himself in Paper and Thought, all the more intelligently intelligent he was, and that intelligence of his, multiplied by itself and a-straddled on itself, was becoming so Intelligent that Jesus Maria!

And here Pyckal and the Baron into my ear: "Yoicks, yoicks!" Likewise the Counsellor from the other side: "Yoicks, yoicks, sick him, yoicks!" Say I: "I am not a dog." Whispered the Counsellor: "Sick him, else Shame for he is their most Famous Author and it cannot be that they Celebrate him when the Great Polish Author, Genius is in the room! Bite him, you chitsh.t, you genius, bite him for if not, we will bite you!" . . . Now behind me stand all my Brood . . . I perceived that there is no other Remedy but that I must bite him else my Countrymen will give me no peace; and if I were to bite that Bison, on this ground a Lion I would remain. But how to bite if the beast as if from a book is Marzipanning, marzipanning so that it sickeneth, and all the more Intelligently Intelligent he is, subtly Subtle . . .

Whereupon I commented to my neighbour, and quite loudly so that he there would hear: "I don't like Butter too Buttery, Noodles too Noodly, Millet too Millety and Barley too Barley!"

This comment of mine, in the general quietude as a Trumpet sounded and to me the general attention turned; and that Rabbi his celebration interrupted, and having set his glasses at me, at me with them from his dark room he peered; whereupon quietly accosted his Neighbour: "Who might that be?" Says the neighbour: "A Foreign Author." Whereupon he became a bit discountenanced and asked whether English, French, or perchance Dutch; but the Neighbour says to him: "A Pole." "A Pole!" he exclaimed, "A Pole! A Pole!" . . . and thereupon, having adjusted his Hat, mightily grimaced with his leg, and then amongst his notes, Papers rummages and says, yet only to His Own, not to me:

"Here they say that butter is buttery . . . The thought interesting indeed . . . an interesting Thought . . . Pity, not quite new for Sartorius already said it in his Bucolics."

They commenced clucking, his answer savouring as if 'twere the finest Marzipan. Yet, clucking, they as if their own clucking contemn, and for this reason that Clucking of theirs falls off. When he to His Own had turned, I in anger to My Own turned and say: "What the devil do I need to know what Sartorius said if I Say?!"

Ergo my own applauded me instantly: "Hail, hail, our Master! He bit him back smartly! Long live Genius Gombrowicz!" Now they applaud, but as if contemning that Applause of theirs . . . so anon it Fell off. Then that one in books, papers fumbled, mightily hashed his leg about, and still only to His Own speaking: "Here they say: What do I care for Sartorius if I Say. And this is not a bad Thought, indeed it could be served with Raisin sauce, but the trouble is that Madame de Lespinasse said something like it in one of her Letters."

Again they cluck, savour, though that Clucking, Savouring of theirs they contemn . . . and in Distraction there is a falling off. Thereupon I turn to My Own so as to answer him Soundly and Bite so that he would not wish to bark again! And here I see: My Own red as Flame; viz. Red as a beetroot the Counsellor, red Pyckal along with the Baron, and Cieciszowski up to his ears in a deep Blush just stands! Oh God, what's that, why were they so suddenly aflame? Indeed, a moment ago they were Admiring, wherefore such a metamorphosis . . . But naught, they stand, Reddening . . . I as if whacked in the Chops for that Countrymen's Blush the which Emblushed me so that suddenly before people all red I have become as if in just a Shirt! The Devil take it! The Devil! Reddened now even my Ears!

Ergo that Mortification of mine that I as a chitsh.t, Red, as if barefoot, cap in hand, at a fence standing; and the worst is that not for the reason of any Shame of mine but a blush of Not Mine though My Own. In fear, then, that through these chitsh.ts of mine who think me a chitsh.t, I'll shew myself a chitsh.t to those other chitsh.ts and, wanting to crush that Chitsh.t, I shouted: "Sh.t! Sh.t! Sh.t!"

He replied: "Ergo 'tis not a bad Thought and good with Mushrooms, just fry it a bit and baste with Cream; but alas, it has already been said by Cambronne . . . " And, in his greatcoat enclosing himself, he made grimaces with his leg.

I was left with no words for I had lost my tongue! And the scoundrel, he had made me mute so that I had no Words as what is mine is not Mine, apparently Stolen!

So stand I in front of all those people and there My Own from behind give me cuffs, tug at me, drag me away, and perchance Red, Red they are . . . Yet here before me those other ones lavish respect on their freak, though at the same time, as if neglecting their respect, they are inspecting socks, shirts, pins. Now heedless of everything, leaving everything, from my disgrace, shame escaping, towards the door through the whole salon I began to go walking, and I Walk Off! I walk off, as the Devil with it all and the Devil, the Devil, all gone to the Devil! Fleeing, walking out I am! But, having walked almost to the door in my open escape, the Devil, the Devil, I think, why the Devil am I fleeing! Why escape? I turned back and return. Through the whole salon I go and all give way to me! The Devil! The Devil! The Devil with it . . . Satan!

So on I go, and I would crack heads, oh I would! But having walked to the wall, I turn again and again back to the door I started for methinks, better not to crack. Yet when I had walked almost to the door, again I turned (for this Walking of mine is already transforming into just a walk across the Salon), and again through the salon I go . . . Now in common amazement, mouths agape, they stare and perchance think me a Halfwit, but the Devil, the Devil, I care not for aught and on I Walk as if I were alone here, and here no one else! And more and more my walk strengthens, becomes Mightier . . . and so the Devil, the Devil, I Walk on and Walk forth and Walk, and so am Walking, Walking and Walking and Walking . . .

And so on I Walk! They throw glances because perchance no one has ever Walked in such a way at a Reception . . . ergo, there by the walls as squirrels they crouched; this one or that crept under Upholstery, or guarded himself with a piece of Furniture . . . and now on I Walk, Walk, and not just Walk but Walking the Devil of a Walk so that haply I'll Crack all . . . oh, Jesus Maria! So now My Own not mine, tail between legs, pack up their drums; they look and I Walk, Walk still, Walk on, whereupon that Walk of mine drums as on a bridge. The Devil, the Devil, and I know not what to do with this Walking of mine, for such a Walk, such a Walk, and I as if uphill Walk, am Walking, and hard, hard, uphill, uphill, oh what a Walk! Oh, what am I doing? Oh, now haply as a Madman I Walk and Walk and Walk, but they will think me a Lunatick . . . yet I Walk, Walk . . . and the Devil, the Devil, Walk, Walk . . .

And now I look and there by the Fireplace someone likewise goes walking, and Walks and Walks. And he so Walks and Walks that when I Walk he likewise Walks. So I from wall to wall and he there from Fireplace to Window . . . and when I walk, he Walks too . . . The Devil take me: why has he stuck thus? What would he? Perchance he is Mocking? . . . Why does he Walk as I do? Yet I could not stop Walking.

Now out of their very fear, they would belike him and me by the pates—out! . . . Although in fear and in Fury, that fury and fear of theirs they slight, ergo it Falls off . . . and although one became pale, the other frowned, the third even his Fist shewed, at the same time petits fours and buns with ham they eat and one to the other: "Is that revista out yet?"—"And I acquired some Tiles for myself . . . "—"I am publishing a new volume of Poetry" . . . Ergo, they Talk thus, Talk, although they are Furious and perchance Afraid, but I see too that they Scoff, and though there one with a bun, the other perchance with a glass, and behind stools, under stools, Angry they are, Talking they are, Afraid They Are, but likewise perchance Scoffing they are . . . and I Walk, Walk, and he likewise there Walks, is Walking and the Devil, the Devil! . . .

So think I, and what is't, and how and why has that man so adhered to me? . . . And more intently I look him over . . . I look him over and see a man of seemly height, very Dark, and of not at all dull, indeed quite noble visage . . . But red lips he has! Lips he has, I say, Red, made Red, Carmined! And so with Lips Red he walks forth, is Walking, Walking! And 'tis as if someone gave me a whack in the Chops! And I as a Crab reddened! So as Boiled, Red, that Walk of mine, the Devil, the Devil, I directed to the door, and through that door—oh, now I'm not Walking on, Walking on but only Walking out . . . Walking—as if the Devil, as if Satan were chasing me—Out!

Cursed that warp of Mankind! Cursed that swine of ours wallowing in mud! Cursed that Slough of ours! Indeed that one who Walked there, with whom I Walked, was no Bull, but a cow!

A Man who, being a Man, fain would not be a Man but after Men chases, and after them Flies, admires, oh, Loves, Heats for them, Lusts for them, Hungers for them, makes up to them, simpers, adulates them, him folk hereabouts give the contemptuous name "puto." Upon seeing those lips, the which although a Man's with woman's rouge bled, I could have no trace of doubt that my lot was to have happen to me a Puto. It was he and I who before all Walked, Walked as in a couple forever coupled!

No surprise then that as a Madman, down the stairs from my shame I fled. But when I run thus along the streets I hear the Running of someone behind, and thus Running hear someone running behind me; and no one else that was but Puto who caught me by the sleeve. "Oh!" he cried. "I know your contempt and know that you my secret have discovered," (and his lips red) "but know you that in me a Friend you have and an Admirer for by your walk you prevailed over all . . . And likewise together with you I began to Walk there so as to be of some Support to you, and so as you wouldn't be one against all . . . Let us walk on then, Walk on!" (Saying this he took me by the arm and his breath—man's but woman's—singes me.) I drew back as in that confusion and consternation of mine I knew not what he would and what asks for, or perchance Lusts for, and besides, I felt a shame before people (though empty the street). But he breaks out laughing and like a woman, thinly, squealing, cries: "Be you not afear'd. You are already too old for me; with Young ones only I sport—with Boys!" So disdained, in choler I pushed him away, but he tenderly pressed against me: "Let us walk on, walk on, walk you with me; together we shall Walk a while! . . . " I naught to this. Yet, since we were going along the street together, he began to tell me His:

Whereupon in a whisper he tells me his all, and I Listen. Viz. that man, perchance Mestizo, Portuguese, of a Persian-Turkish mother in Libya born, was called Gonzalo; and very Rich; about eleven or twelve in the morning from his bed gets up, drinks coffee, and then walks out into a street and there along it goes and after Youths or Lads. When he has singled out one, anon comes up to him, asks the way; and having thus begun with him starts to chat about this and that just to gather if that Boy can be persuaded into sin for five, ten, or even fifteen Pesos. But most often in Fear, in Terror he dared not speak of it, and they shunned him, whereupon he would away as if Stepped on. So then after another Boy, Youth, or even Lad who caught his eye . . . and there, if you please, again about the way asking, talking, and again about some Games or Dances chatting and all to tempt one for fifteen or twenty pesos; yet that Boy might say a sharp word to him or spit. Then he flees, but in Heat. Now after another Brunet or a Blond, accosting, inquiring. Then when he tires, he comes back to his home to rest and there on the Sopha having rested a bit, again onto a street to look for, walk, approach, ask now a Craftsman, now a Labourer or an Apprentice, or a Scullery Lad or a Soldier, or a Sailor. Most often though in Horror, Fear, whenever forth he steps, Back he steps straight; or else, if you please, he goes after one and that one has gone into a Shop or from sight has sunk away and naught on't. Again then to his home, tired, fatigued, but Afire, comes back and having supped and rested on the Sopha, again into a street dashes, a Boy, if only well-shaped, to single out, talk into't. If then he came by such a one and has settled on terms for ten, fifteen, or twenty Pesos, straightway to his lodging leads him; and there, having locked the door with a key, he his jacket, tie, trousers doffs, drops on the Floor, undresses down to his Shirt and the light dims, Perfume sprays. And here the Lad him in the jaw and to the Wardrobe to seize his linen or snatch his Cashes! Numb from a terrible fear Puto dares not cry out, allows him to take all and suffers his painful blows. From those Blows, Cuffs, his Heat even stronger! So after the Lad has left, he again into the street, blazing, Flaming, enraptured and likewise Terrified, Anguished, and on after Apprentices, young Craftsmen, Soldiers or Sailors; but whenever forth he steps, Back he steps for, although the lust great, the Fear greater than the lust. But now the night is late and streets are more and more empty; then to his home comes Puto back, down to his Shirt undresses, his tired bones in bed, lonely, comforts, so that tomorrow would Get up, drink coffee, and after Young boys chase—again. And the next day again he gets up, trousers, jacket dons, and after Young boys chases again. And the next day, having got up from his Bed, again into a street so as after Boys to chase.

Whereupon I say: "Is't possible, you miserable man, that a Craftsman or an Apprentice or a Soldier can yield to your temptation if only Disgust, Abomination you can rouse in him by your charms?" No sooner had I said this does he cry and seemingly sore wounded: "You are mistaken 'cause Eyes large and Fiery I have, and a white hand, and a Delicate foot!" Anon a few steps forth he ran, his Figure in undulations and gallantries displaying to me and Mincing it smartly. But thereupon he says: "After all, they are in need; coppers they need!" "Why, though," say I, "why do you not give them more cashes, but only ten, fifteen, or twenty pesos, if you are rich and it costs you so much trouble to persuade?" Replies he: "Look at my clothes. I as an ordinary Sales clerk or a Barber dress and wear a shirt for eight Pesos, and this only so as not to betray my Riches; for by now I might have been perchance ten times suffocated, or with a Knife, or my Pate made hash of; and if I were to give a Boy more Pesos he would straight ask for more and then intrusion of my home, Threatening, Menacing, just to squeeze, cheat some more out of me. This is why, although a palace I have, my own Lackey I pretend to be. And my own Lackey I am in my Palace!"

Here he cried in a desperate voice, but Shrilly: "Cursed, cursed that Fate of mine!" But anon raising towards the sky his hands—or dainty hands perchance—he cried Shrilly, piercingly: "Blessed, oh sweet, Marvellous my fate and I wish no other!" In tiny steps forth through the Air he strides and I alongside, trotting as in a Chaise. To the right, to the left he eyes with an eye large, wet, languid, and I alongside as Horse by Mare! Now giggles with a tinkling, now tears, large and womanly, sheds, and I here, markye, just as at a Tartar wedding!

Suddenly into a side street he darted and along it runs for he had caught sight of a Soldier . . . but anon he stops, dodges around a corner as an Apprentice was passing . . . now again from the corner darts out after a Sales clerk and stops again, peers around, edges around back-ways and this 'cause a Scullery Lad passed, robust, young . . . And so by young Boys tossed, by them as by Dogs on all sides torn, now to the right, now to the left rushes, courses, and I behind him . . . for now he draws me along! And his Sin, Dark, Black, gave me some relief from this terrible shame of mine that I had swallowed at the Reception. And in darkness, in Sin we burst onto a Plaza where the tower built by the English is: there a hill inclines towards a river and the city descends to the port, and soft the river's tone as a tune amidst the Plaza's trees . . . There many young Sailors were.

But she, who after one of them has just been coursing, stopped as if struck by a Thunderbolt. "Do you see that Boy, that

Blond there ahead of us? It must be a miracle or even an Omen of good fortune! Him I love more than all others; after him I have already betimes rushed, dashed but he ever disappeared from my sight. Oh bliss, joy that I see him again; again after him, after him, ah, after him can run!"

And, heedless of everything now, after this Youth darted; and I behind him! From a distance I could not see much of that Blond Boy and only his jacket, his head glimpsed . . . but I see that he makes towards the gates of a park, with cheap merrymaking for the common folk, the which is called Japanese Park and the which on one side of the Plaza with garish lamps is lighted, and there he stopped in the flickering glare of lanterns, the which from boards, posts hung. Ergo, he stands there as if waiting. And she amidst the trees that were on the Plaza like a Weasel ran and, in their shadow taking cover, from there began to yearn towards him and sigh.

Ergo methinks: And what is't? Where am I? What do I do? And from him would I have fled long ago, yet sorrowful sore was I to desert my only companion. For a Companion he was. Yet, when by the Tree he so together with me, I feel somewhat discomfited as neither Fish nor Fowl. Viz. hairs black, manly he had on his hand, but this hand—Dimpled, White, dainty Hand . . . and likewise perchance foot . . . and although a Cheek dark with shaven hairs, this Cheek of his charms and coquettes as if 'twere not Dark but indeed white . . . and likewise Leg though Manly as if 'twould be a Dainty leg and Charms in curious caprices . . . and though head of a man in his prime, bald at the brow, Wrinkled, this head as if slips off a head, seeking to be a dainty head . . . So he as if fain would not himself, and himself Transforms in the silence of the night, and now you wit not whether 'tis He or She . . . and perchance, being neither this nor that, he has the aspect of a Creature and not a human . . . He lurks, the rascal, stands, says naught, and only at his Boy silently gazes. So I think, what the Devil, Werewolf, and wherefore I here with him when he Shames me and because of him my disgrace at that Reception, but the Devil, Satan, and be it the Devil himself, I will not desert him in any case since he walked with me and so together we Walk.

Suddenly a Man older, grizzled, to that Boy came up; upon seeing this, Puto became exceeding agitated, has begun to give me signs and says: "This curse, this Misfortune of mine! Who is that Old codger? What would he with him? Surely they were appointed to meet here and he will treat him! . . . Go you thither, listen to what they are saying to each other . . . Go you thither, listen, for I am dying with jealousy . . . go, go . . . "

His whisper, hot, well-nigh singed my ear. Having emerged from under the trees, I came closer to the Youth who, of middling height, fair hair, foot, hand of middling size and those eyes of his so, Teeth so, Crown so—that rascal, rascal, oh rascal Gonzalo! But what do I hear! Our Tongue indeed!

As if burnt, I quickly away from them sprang and forth to Gonzalo: "Do as you will. But I'm off and naught I'll have with it since they are my Countrymen and belike Son with Father! Naught, and home I'll go!"

By the hand he has seized me: "Oh!" he does cry, "God had it so that you happened to me, my Friend, and you will not refuse me your support! And if they are your Countrymen it will be easy for you to make acquaintance with them! And then you will acquaint me with them and I'll be your wholehearted Friend for all time, and even ten, twenty, thirty thousand will give you or haply more! Let us walk on, walk on after them—they are already entering the Park!"

I would Beat him! But he comes closer, presses against me: "Let's walk on, walk on, for indeed together we Walk. Walk you, walk you, let us Walk on, Walk on!" And so saying he started forward, and I to my Walking, went into my Walk, and let's Walk on, Walk on, Walk on!

So into the park we run! And there trains with a roar from behind a Cliff, yonder Harlequins or empty Bottles, else Carousels or See-saws, or Trampolines; further on a-circling on wooden horses, a-shooting at target, a make-believe Grotto or Curved Mirrors and so everything, if you please, in the din of Merrymaking and amidst Chinese lanterns, sky Rockets and Fire-works, turns, flies, shoots! And people walk and just know not—one looks at a See-saw, another at a Harlequin and so from a Mirror to a Bottle walks and gapes either at this or at that; and everything galloping, vibrating, here a Monster and there a Hypnotist! So the merriment bubbles, See-saws swing, Carousels chase their tails, and people are walking, walking and walking, and walking and walking, and from a See-saw to a Carousel else from a Carousel to a See-saw. So turn the Carousels. Swing the See-saws. And people are just Walking. And Mirrors lure with lanterns, Bottles shout with a barker's voice, and so if not Bottles then a Train that bursts with a roar, or a Lake in the make-believe grotto, or a Harlequin; from which Glare and Roar and all merriments', Amusements' turning and whirling and flying. And whilst Amusements Amuse themselves, people are walking, walking!

~

Running headlong was Gonzalo, afraid they might be lost to him in the crowd and, having found them, he made signs at me to come apace. And to me: "They are going into the Dance Hall!" I say: "We'd do better to go round on the Carousel." He says: "No, no, into the Dance Hall!" Whereupon into the Dance Hall. There two orchestras that play alternately. There, in the limitless space, mayhap a thousand tables aswarm with people, and in the midst the great surface of the floor Lake-hued. Then the Music plays, whereupon couples come out, turn; and when the Music stops, the couples stop alike. So vast the hall, so great its space that from one end to the other—as in the Mountains when from a height, the highland, the eye in a Valley there strays, drowns—people like unto ants . . . and from the distance comes a Hum, and the voice of music strays. Workers, maids, vendors, apprentices, and Sailors aplenty, and Soldiers, also clerks, seamstresses, or Vendeuses, and by the tables they sit or in the midst turn themselves to the time of the music; when the Music breaks off, they stop. The hall exceeding white.

The youth with his father ('cause it was his father) was sitting at a table and drinking beer. We with Gonzalo sat at the neighbouring table and Gonzalo ever after me to make their acquaintance. "Go to them, drink to them as Fellow countrymen and I will belike Drink, and drink together in Company we will!"

But the hall large, lights galore, and people stare so I feel Uneasy and say: "Not to do for 'tis too impertinent" . . . and in my mind I was seeking a reason to take leave as Ashamed I was even to sit with such a man at the table. He importunes, I demur. We are supping wine, and the Music plays and the couples turn. Whereupon Gonzalo again that I should go to them and as besotted glances at his Chosen one and, trying to endear himself and catch his eye, he winks, flutters his hand (his Dainty hand), giggles, and jiggles his seat . . . and then, Poking a waiter with his elbow, "More wine!" he shouts and likewise makes little bread pellets and shoots them, greeting these Pranks of his with riotous laughter! And more and more embarrassed as now people begin looking, say I: "For necessity I needs must go," and I go to the Privy; and that with the intention of escaping his sight and being lost. To the Privy I am going, going . . . But someone in the crowd caught me by the sleeve. And who? Pyckal! Behind Pyckal the Baron and after him Ciumkała! At this my Bewilderment. How came they here?! And I wonder if they are not spoiling for a Brawl as perchance they have hastened here after me to have at me for that shame, the which they had swallowed at the Reception . . . But naught of that!

"Ah, Pan Witold, dear, Esteemed! So we meet again! So let's go and Drink a dram! A dram! Let's to it, I'll treat! No, no, I'll Treat! No, no, I'll Treat!"

Instantly Pyckal bawled: "What think you, dunce—you will Treat! Did you see the dolt! I'll Treat!" But the Baron takes me by the arm, leads me aside, and Whirrs hard, buzzes as a Bumblebee: "Listen not to them, Pan. Ears burn from such Boorishness.

We will drink something Together. Prithee, prithee, my Pan!" But Pyckal caught me by the sleeve and draws me away and into my ear says: "Why should that French Poodle bore you with his Silly, Idiotic airs? Come you with me. We will Drink, and with no Ceremony!"

Say I then: "God reward you, God reward you. There is no greater honour for me than to drink with you, friends of mine. But I'm in Company."

As I have said this, they nudge each other with their elbows, and likewise wink, nod their heads: "In company, in company! In Company, indeed! And belike with Gonzalo you are, the Devil! You have befriended Gonzalo, with Gonzalo you Walk, may I be kicked by a Duck! But that man sits on millions! You are not as mad as people say. Let's go for a dram! for a dram! Let's drink, I'll Treat! No, no, I'll Treat!"

So they are more and more cordially, familiarly approaching, but since they do not dare nudge me with the elbow, they nudge each other under the ribs, they poke each other, they banter amongst themselves and now each to the others: "Let's go, let's drink!" All that as if for themselves but perchance for me . . . and they have now begun to Hug, kiss each other (viz. with me they would not dare) and "Let's go, Let's go! I'll treat. No, no, I'll treat!" Pyckal shakes his Purse; the Baron his likewise; Ciumkała his cashes takes out of a wrapper. Now each shews his to the others, each sticks his cashes under the nose of the others. And Pyckal called out: "You'll not Treat me; I'll treat you and, what's more, I may give you some hundred pesos if I feel so inclined!" The Baron exclaimed: "I will give you even two hundred!" And Ciumkała: "I have three hundred here, here I have three hundred and further fifteen in coins!"

I see that, although they are treating each other thus, each other inviting and shewing these cashes each to the others, perchance me they would Treat and perchance me they would shew . . . except that they dare not . . . and haply they suspect me of an Amour with the exceeding rich Puto . . . and for this reason perchance they would give me heaps of gold, and they know not themselves with what to treat me, how to plead with me! At such a heavy insult and likewise shame that they seemingly see a lover of his in me . . . I nearly whacked a mug, but just cried not to pother my brain, there being no time! . . . and I quickly made off. I enter the Privy, they after me. There was one man who was making water into a Urinal. I to a urinal, they to urinals. But when that man who had been making water left, they jointly at me. And the Baron shouted to Pyckal: "Here, have five hundred Pesos." And Ciumkała to the Baron: "Here, have six hundred." And Pyckal to Ciumkała: "Here seven hundred, have seven hundred. Take when I'm giving!" They take cashes out, brandish them under noses for themselves, for me, and press them each on the others! Haply they are Madmen!

I reckoned then that, although they are giving these Cashes each to the others amongst themselves, they would fain give me these Cashes to purchase my favour . . . save that they feel awkward for want of daring with me. Ergo I say: "Do not fever yourselves, Gentles, easy, easy." Yet they were but seeking a way to press these Cashes on me, and at length the Baron clasped his head: "Aye me, my pocket is torn. I'd better give my Cashes to you as I may lose them!" . . . and he started to press the Cashes on me. Seeing that, the others also press theirs: "My pocket is torn, too. Take mine"—"And mine." Say I: "For God's sake, gentles, to what end do you give?" . . . But at this moment someone came in for the need, so they to Urinals, unbutton, whistle, as if naught, as if for the need . . . Only when that someone who had come in went out, they at me again, and since they have become more daring, they indeed thrust the Cashes on me and "Take, take," they chorus. Say I: "In the name of the Father and the Son, gentlemen, to what end do you give, what purpose you your cashes with me?" In this moment, however, someone came in for the need, so they to Urinals, whistle . . . but as soon as we were left alone, again they lept at me and Pyckal roared: "Take, take when you are given, take, take for he has three hundred or four hundred Millions!"—"Take not from Pyckal; take from me," cried the Baron, whirring and buzzing as a wasp, "from me take, as, for God's sake, he may have even four hundred or five hundred Millions!"

And Ciumkała moaned, whimpered, sighed: "Perchance even six hundred Millions—take, I beg you the favour, Your Honor, likewise my pittance!" Whilst each, reddened, heated, so insists and waves these Cashes, pressing them, thrusting them on me, the first nigh the second and the third, the first hard upon the second, upon the third, they Together amongst Themselves—at me, at me. Wishing not to be disagreeable any longer, I let them press the Cashes on me. Then all to Urinals as someone was just coming in. I with these Cashes towards the door and from the Privy rushed out into the dance hall; and there music plays, couples turn. I with these Cashes stopped. I see that my Gonzalo at the table is still pranking and pranking and pranking . . .

Now he waves his Dainty hand; flutters his eyelashes; then bread Pellets he tosses; now he tinkles his glass; now he clasps fingers to his cheek, and so he amongst these pranks of his as a Turkey amongst Sparrows . . . with riotous laughter his own Pranks salutes! So those, who were sitting near him, perchance thought him in his cups, but I knew what was that Wine of his and to whom he directs those pranks. Although I in abomination would fain go home, flee, Leave off, this sight pricks me as a knife (and now tossing his Heel up) for (and now fluttering his handkerchief) a comrade of mine 'tis, an ally (clapping his palms, clapping his knees) with whom I had walked (wiggling his fingers); thus I cannot for myself allow him such a spectacle of himself to make in the presence of others (piping on a paper pipe). Ergo, back to the table I directed myself.

Upon seeing me, out of prank he began waving at me, beckoning me. Thereupon, when I came closer, he exclaimed: "Heigh heigh, sit you, sit, we'll make Merry! Heigh heigh, heigh heigh, sunny Honey!

Honey, honey is Pankracy,
But my sweeting is Ignacy!

And a pellet thrusts at my nose, paper he pipes, and softly says: "You traitor, where have you been, what have you been doing? This matter of mine is Tedious for you!" And anon likewise his Glass of wine clinks against mine, deals napkins about, and pours wine into a glass for me. "Let's drink! Let's drink!"

Mother forbids the dance
And still I do prance!

"So let's merry-make! Let's rejoice!" He pours wine for me. I cannot refuse as he urges boisterously. We drink. But next to us, at another table, the Baron, Pyckal, Ciumkała have seated themselves and call for wine! To the Devil! It seems that, since they have given me Cashes, they feel more daring and when Gonzalo takes sips, they likewise to Tankards, to glasses; with Tankards, Glasses, Mugs they clink, they Drink, they Down, they shout, Heigh heigh, nonny no—heigh for a rainy day, oh! They had not enough daring, though, to drink to us, so they drank to themselves only. We with Gonzalo likewise to each other would drink.

Thine Eye that shines so
Shoot quick, he comes ho.

But quietly he says: "Go to the Old Gentleman, invite them to our company. We will get acquainted."

Say I: "It cannot be."

Under the table he presses something into my hand and says: "Take it, take it. Have it. Keep it . . ." and Cashes these were. "Take," says he. "You have need. Recognize a Friend, an Admirer, and if you care to be a Friend to me I will a Friend be to you!" I am loathe to take but he is pressing forcefully and so impresses. Markye, I would have dashed these Cashes on the floor but, since I had already had those Cashes and now to those new ones were added, I know not what to do as belike some four thousand has already amassed.

The while the Baron and his comrades drank amongst themselves, but they began Drinking to me likewise. With their cashes in pocket, I could do them no less than drink to them; so they again drink to me; Gonzalo drinks to me; I to Gonzalo; they to Gonzalo; Gonzalo to them! We drink, drink on. Merrymaking indeed!

Oh, Kisser, why kiss me?
My lips are not for thee!

Paper he pipes; hand, foot he flutters! Hoopla, hoopla! So now we all together each to the others from one table to the other drink. But to tell the truth, not to these but to those Gonzalo drank, viz. to the old Gentleman and to the Son. Says he to me likewise: "Go, bid their company!"

Whereupon I rise and, to the old gentleman having come up, these words I uttered: "Forgive me, Pan, such intrusiveness, but I have heard our tongue so I wish to greet my Countrymen."

At once most politely having risen, he introduced himself as "Kobrzycki Tomasz, formerly Major, now Retired," and likewise a son of his, Ignacy, introduced. Then he asks me to be seated. I did alight; he proffers beer. But I could see that my company was not quite to his taste, and that for the reason of those Companions of mine. And chiefly that they there Yell, Drink, Roar! Upon seeing then that exceeding upright, honest man, in these words I speak: "I am in company, but they appear a bit beliquored, and 'tis known to you, Esteemed Gentleman, that no one chooses acquaintances here; oft 'twould be better if Acquaintances could turn into Non-acquaintances!"

And there they Roar. But says he: "I am aware of your constrained situation and, if 'twould please you, take more peaceable merriment with us." Ergo we go on Discoursing. This man exceeding worthy, Decent was, of Dry features, well-proportioned, grizzly head, fair eye, grey and very Bushy, of dry countenance but Mossy, voice Mossy too, hand dry and likewise Mossy, nose aquiline but bushy and exceeding Mossy, and alike ears with bunches of hairs, grey and overgrown. His son, a-close now, quite well-moulded, shapely seemed to me; and his hand, foot—so, his teeth, crown—so, that rascal, rascal, oh, rascal Gonzalo! And there they roar, roar out! Herewith the Old Gentleman to me: that to the army he is dispatching his Only Son, the which, if unable to reach our Country, would enlist in England or in France, so that from this side he could wrack the enemy. "Ergo," quoth he, "we happened into this Park so that my Ignacy before his leave-taking could pleasure himself, and some Folk Revels I would have him see." He speaks, and there they are drinking. What then in this man drew attention was some exceeding sense in his speech and all his behaviour, and so sensible, so discreet he was in every word and deed of his that as an Astronomer constantly within himself he Scans, attends. Also exceeding mannerly.

Confronted with such Mannerliness and Sensibleness in all things, such Honourableness, confronted with apparent exceeding purity, righteousness in all Affairs, designs, I am ever more ashamed of those Companions of mine and of my own affairs and petty affairs. But not desiring to confess to him these vexations of mine, I say just this: "Your worthy aim I wish the best, Honoured Sir; permit me to drink with One's Son to the success of those worthy, Noble plans." So we clinked. But when I clinked with the Son, there likewise Gonzalo drank to me. And likewise the Baron, Pyckal, Ciumkała drank to me. Hoopla, hoopla, hoopla, let's drink, let's rejoice! Ergo, I needs drink to them; they to me. Then the Old Gentleman:

"Well, then, I see they are drinking."

"Indeed, they are."

"They are drinking to you."

"They are, for our acquaintance."

He mused, he saddened . . . and at last he said a bit lower: "Oh, methinks, 'tis not the Time for such frolics . . . not the Time . . . "

I am ashamed! Whereupon, bending to his ear, in these words quietly did I speak: "Zounds, you'd best go from here together with this son of yours, and I'm telling you this out of friendship 'cause they are Drinking, but not to me!"

The Old Man frowned: "And to whom are they drinking?"

Say I: "To that Foreigner, Companion of mine they drink, yet he not to them or to me but to that Son of yours."

Astounded, he bristled: "To Ignasio he drinks? What means this?"

"To Ignasio, to Ignasio. And hie thee hence with thy Ignasio for 'tis Ignasio he is chasing after! Hie thee hence, hie thee hence, I say!"

And here they Bellow, Swill, Toot, Roar, steadily Glasses, tankards, flagons drain! And hoopla, hoopla, and Hansel-Gretel! Racket, clamour as in a market! The Old Man reddened as a Tomato: "I too reckoned that he eyed my Son, but I knew not for what reason."

"Hie thee hence, hie thee hence with your Son else you'll expose yourself to people's raillery!"

"I with Ignacy (and still quietly into the Ear we are talking) will not flee as my Ignacy is not a maiden! For God's sake, mix not Ignacy in this, tell not Ignacy! I myself will deal with that man."

The while to Gonzalo the Baron and Pyckal drink, and Gonzalo towards us waves his handkerchief and downs a mug. "Heigh heigh, be happy; heigh heigh, be jolly!"

The Old Gentleman took hold of his mug as if he would drink to Gonzalo . . . but suddenly he banged this mug on the table. From the table he sprang up! Gonzalo likewise stood up! Whereupon others likewise begin to stand up, having sensed there is about to be a Combat. Only the Son did not move but he was ill at Ease for possibly he reckoned what was rustling in the rushes; and as a shellfish the poor fish blushed.

Ergo, stands the Old Man; and likewise stands Gonzalo. This one despite that effeminacy of his was quite a sizeable man; but when the Smell of Combat wafted, he greatly softened; and so Puto stands aghast and the Old Man stands; Puto stands aghast and the Old Man stands; aghast Puto stands and the Old Man stands. And so it was for quite a while. Gonzalo with the fingers of his left hand lightly, quietly Frolicked, and that as if wagging his tail and asking that everything into a Joke, into a little frolick be turned. But the Old Man stands and Gonzalo has now, out of that fear of his, in dread, in anxiety, a Mug, the which he held in his other hand, to his lips lifted, a Drink taking. Calamity of his! Perchance he has forgotten that but over that very Drinking this jangle is! Now the Old Man's question could be heard:

"To whom drink you?"

To whom indeed? To nobody he drank. He drank out of fear, and he takes not the Mug from his lips, for if he were to take, he would have to answer! So he Drinks, stays Drinking to be Drinking. But the trouble is—the Devil, the Devil—that whilst previously he drank to the Son furtively, now his Drinking again towards the Son itself directs. (The Son at the table sat and did not move.) And so stands Rascal She, Drinks, and to that Boy a little Drinks!

Realizing and fearing the mighty wrath of Tomasz, he has softened as a rag. But indeed out of Fear he drinks the more, and by this Drinking yields himself to Tomasz's Wrath . . . and the more fearing the Wrath, he Drinks and Drinks! Exclaimed Tomasz:

"Ah, to me you drink!"

Yet in sooth not to him he did Drink; but to the Son. Apparently, though, Tomasz had so exclaimed with the intent, viz. to turn from his Son that Drinking of Gonzalo's. There Pyckal, the Baron and Ciumkała were guffawing! Gonzalo glances at the Old Gentleman and drinks on, and although he has already drunk it all, he still drinks and drinks . . . But now he obviously drinks to the Boy, and now with this drinking of his he changes himself into Woman and in Her, in that woman, escape, protection from Tomasz's wrath he finds! For now not a Man! Now a Woman! Exclaimed Tomasz, out of Wrath as a Tomato fearsome:

"I forbid you, Sir, to drink to me; I disallow a Non-acquaintance to drink to me!"

But what Sir is he? Not sir but Madam! And in sooth not to him does drink but to the Son. And Drinks, Drinks, and although the Mug already empty, Drinks, Drinks and so that Drinking of his ad Infinitum lengthens and with Drinking he defends himself, with that Drinking o'erdrinks and drinks and drinks, and ceases not to Drink. Whereupon, since Drink any longer he cannot, when that Drinking for him was over, he took the mug from his lips and threw it at the Old Man!

Crack! Into small chinks the mug shattered above Tomasz's eye!

But Tomasz moves not, just stands. Then the son sprang up but Tomasz exclaimed:

"Stay out, Ignacy!"

And naught, but stands. And blood appears, and one large Drop over his cheek is rolling. Ergo, there is going to be a Combat; they will lock heads . . . So Pyckal, the Baron, Ciumkała from the table did move and began aught to pick up—one a Tankard, the other a Bottle, the third a Club or a Stool; but Tomasz moves not, just stands! Skulls are steaming so 'tis murky! Those who apart did stand edged closer, and now Pyckal, the Baron, not daring to enter Combat with someone there, each other began to rough up and by the Mop, and so perchance cracking Skulls, tearing Ears . . . and my eyes are murky, Hum, Fog, as I had been drinking too. But Tomasz stands. And there appeared the second Drop, the which dribbled along the path of the first one.

I look: but naught. Stands Tomasz and stands Gonzalo. The third Drop slowly dribbled along the path of the first two, and on Tomasz's Waistcoat fell. Merciful God, what is't? Why moves Tomasz not? But he just stands. And a new, fourth Drop dribbled. From Tomasz's silent drops all became silent and Tomasz looks at us and we at Tomasz; and the fifth Drop dribbles.

Trickles, Trickles. We all stand. Gonzalo Moves not. Anon back to his table he went, took his Hat, and slowly made off . . . till his back was lost from our sight. Ergo, when Gonzalo had gone, everybody made a move—took hat, went home, and so everyone cleared away, everything Cleared Away.

That night I was for a long time wakeful. Oh, why have I been obedient to the Legation? Why did I go to that Reception? Why did I Walk at that reception? They will not forgive me that

Shame and possibly I am already ridiculed by all, contemned, a Buffoon proclaimed. And when just one, only one man who denied me not his Recognition, and perchance even some Admiration, turned out to be a Puto, and when he into his courtship drew me as a Pander, what Ignominy and Disgrace of mine! Therewith, tossing in bed I sigh, moan. Oh, Gombrowicz, Gombrowicz, oh, where is that Greatness, that Distinction of yours? Haply you are Distinguished but as a Pander, Great but Friend of a Knave out to undo a Compatriot of yours worthy and good, and also that one's Son young and good. And when there far away, over the waters, blood, here likewise blood; and Tomasz's drops that are for my doing spilt. How this blood of Tomasz's did weigh on me, how in its conjunction with that blood being spilt it did terrify me! And abed buffeted by pain, I felt that blood issuing from blood there, here shed, can lead me to blood heavier still . . .

To break with Gonzalo, to put him from one's own self away . . . Yet we did already Walk together, did Walk, indeed Walk we together, Walk, and how am I to Walk without him if together we walk . . . So passed the night! But when morning came, a strange Thing and so hard, stubborn as if Skull against wall: viz. Tomasz arrives and, having apologized for a call at an early hour, begs me to challenge Gonzalo on his behalf! I was dumbfounded and did say: "Why? To what end? What aim?" Yesterday he put Gonzalo down sufficiently, and how to challenge him, how to duel with him but a Cow . . . Hard, stubborn, he answered me: "Cow or not a cow, wears Breeches and the insult was publick, and it cannot be that I come out of this as a poltroon, and moreover in front of Foreigners!"

Lost, then, my persuasions: how can one with a cow? Challenge a cow? Become prey to tongues and perchance fan new laughter? 'Tis better to hush-hush and keep it under as the shame would be Ignacy's, too. He cried:

"Cow or not a cow, such talk! And not to Ignacy he drank, but to me, the elder! And not at Ignacy he threw the mug, but at me! Betwixt us there was a drunken jangle and an insult, as it happens betwixt Men!"

I to him that Cow. But he will insist and still Cries sharply that Ignacy had nothing to do with this, that that one is not a Cow. Finally he says: "Ergo, I must challenge him. I will duel with him so that this matter in a manly manner betwixt Men is settled; to be sure, I will make a Man of him that it cannot be said that a Puto is after my Son! Ergo, if he does not stand up to me, I will shoot him as a Dog, and you tell him so, so that he knows. He must stand up to me!"

His obstinacy surprised me and 'twas already clear that this man will not rest till he forces Gonzalo into Man; for perchance he could not bear his son's being ridiculed; so, despite the very obvious, he pits himself in this way against the obvious, the which he wishes to change! Yet how force Gonzalo to stand up? Heads together. To me Tomasz said that first I on my own to Gonzalo should go and privately suggest to him that either Port or Transport: viz. either he stands up or risks certain death from Tomasz's hand. Only then was I to go to him the second time, now with a second witness, to Challenge him pro forma.

No Remedy. No good, oh, no good. Perchance 'twould be better to leave off because this doing against the very nature: viz. to challenge a Puto. But despite the obvious, despite reason, some hope was tapping within: that haply he would accept this challenge, stand up a Man. And then for me none such shame that I with him at the reception did walk, and likewise with him to the Japanese Park did walk. Ergo, I'll go, hurl at him this challenge, see what he does do. So (although it smelled Not Good), heedful of Tomasz's plea, I betook myself to Gonzalo.

I arrived at the palace, the which, behind a large gilded grate, abandonment, emptiness emitted. A long while outside the door I was made to wait, and when at last it opened, there Gonzalo stood, but in a lackey's Apron, White, with a floor Broom and a rag. I recollected that he out of fear of the Boys, those boys of his, was wont to feign his own lackey, but naught, I Enter, he recoils: paled and his arms did flop as a Rag. Only when I said that I had come to Chat with him, did he turn a bit easeful and says: "Of course, of course, but let us go to my Closet where we can better chat." Through chambers large, gilded, to the Closet he leads me the which Dirty, God forbid, and there was nary even a bed there, only a Pallet on bare boards. On the pallet he sits and to me: "What's out there? What news out there?" Whereupon I Spat.

His ears blanched. He flopped and as a rag drooped. Say I:

"You are challenged to a duel by the Aged Gentleman whom you have insulted. Swords or pistols."

He turned quiet, keeps quiet, whereupon I tell him: "You are challenged to a duel."

"I am challenged to a duel?!"

"Aye, you are," say I, "challenged to a duel!"

"I am challenged to a duel?!"

He squealed very thinly, fluttered dainty hands, glanced with that eye of his, and said in that Dainty voice of his: "I am challenged to a duel?"

Whereupon say I: "Leave off that Dainty voice, leave off that Eye, that dainty hand, and best fulfil your obligation! And out of friendship I am telling you this, for know you that if you stand not up to Tomasz, he has sworn to kill you as a Dog. Port or Transport."

I thought he would cry out but he only Yielded as a rag and his large feet on the floor enfeebled lie; and black hairs that he has on his hand likewise enfeebled thus, yielded as if of Down. Transfixed, at me with an Ox-eye as a Cow he looks. I asked: "What you to this?" He says naught, but enfeebled, enfeebled as a Drenched Hen and only when he has thus Enfeebled does he, languidly as a Chinese Queen, stretch himself and murmur sweetly:

"And all for Ignasiek, my Ignasiek!"

Out of fear then he enfeebled into Woman and when Woman, he is afraid no more! 'Cause what is a duel to a Woman! I was still trying to speak to his sense and say I: "Think you, Arturo, that you insulted the Old Gentleman (he cried: The Old Man's a fig!) who will not allow his Honour to be racked (he cried: Honour's a fig!), and moreover, in the presence of other compatriots of his (he cried: Compatriots—a fig!), and I myself will not let you not stand up to this Father (he cried: Father's a fig!), and likewise tell you to drum the Son out of your head" (he cries: The Son's the thing, oh, indeed!).

Weeps; and weeping he moans: "I thought you were a Friend to me since I am to you a friend. How did that old gent o'erturn you? Instead of siding with the old Father, with the Young Ones you'd best join, to the Young Ones some freedom give, and the Young One from Pan Father's Tyranny protect!"

~

Speaks he: "Come hither; I've something to tell you."

Say I: "From afar I hear well enough."

Says he: "Hither come; I would tell you something."

Say I: "Why hither if I can hear?"

Says he: "Haply I would tell you something, but into your ear."

Say I: "No need into the ear. We are alone."

Yet speaks he: "I know that you hold me a Monster. Albeit I will give you cause to be on my side against that Father and acknowledge such ones as I the Salt of the Earth. Tell me: do you not acknowledge Progress? Are we to step in place? And how can there be aught New if just to the Old you give credence? Eternally then is Pan Father to hold a young son under his paternal lash? Eternally then is a Young One to rattle off prayers after Pan Father? Give some slack to the Young One, let him out free rein, let him frisk!"

Speak I: "You madman! For progress I am too, but you call Deviation progress."

Replied he to this: "But if to deviate a bit, well?"

Whereupon, after he thus spoke, say I: "I'faith, you may tell this to such ones as you yourself are, and not to a man decent and honourable. I would not be a Pole if I were to set a Son against a Father; know you that we Poles our Fathers respect exceedingly, and thus you do not tell a Pole that he should a Son from a Father and, moreover, for Deviation take." Exclaimed he: "But wherefore need you be a Pole?"

Further says he: "Has the lot of the Poles up to now been so delightful? Has not your Polishness become loathsome to you? Have you not had your fill of Sorrow? Your fill of Soreness, Sadness? And today they are flaying your skins again! And you insist so on staying in that skin of yours? Would you not become something Else, something New? Would you have all these Boys of yours but just repeat everything forever after Fathers? Oh, release Boys from the paternal cage. Let them veer off the path, let them peer into the Unknown! Thus far the old Father that colt of his has ridden bare and guided according to his own design . . . and now let the colt take the bit between the teeth so that he carries his Father where he will! And then the Father's eyes will nigh whiten for his own Son doth carry him, carry him away! Gee-up, go! Give free rein to those Boys of yours, let them Gallop, let them Run, let them Bolt and be Carried away!"

Thereupon I cried: "Be still! Cease that Importuning of yours as 'tis impossible for me to be against the Father and the land of our fathers, against Pater and Patria, and what's more, in a moment such as the present!" Mutters he: "To the Devil with Pater and Patria! The Son, the son's the thing, oh, indeed! But wherefore need you Patria? Is not Filistria better? You exchange Patria for Filistria and then you'll see!"

When he mentioned that "Filistria" I, in that first choler of mine, would fain have struck him; but this word so unwise to my ear sounded that at that Sick and haply Mad man laughter overtook me, and so I Laugh, Laugh . . . albeit he mutters:

"What about that old Gent? But you press so that perchance I would (out of friendship I am telling you so) stand up to him in a duel. I'faith, I would stand up if I had as a witness to the duel a trusted Friend who would slip bullets into sleeve at the loading of pistols. Give up the old Gent! What's the Old Gent to you? Let the Old Man shoot only with powder: thus the Wolf is full and the Goat is whole. And after the duel a reconciliation can be made, and even a Draught taken! When I bravely stand up to him and shew myself a Man then he haply will not forbid me with that Ignasiek of his-mine to drink . . . "

I again into laughter; for indeed Laughable that thought of his; but speak I: "Not just one witness loads the arms; there are other witnesses."

Says he: "Why need they mark it? It can be smoothly contrived since 'tis not the first time a duel with Bullets into Sleeve." I at that: "And if they fall to the ground out of the Sleeve?"

Speaks he: "Into the sleeve an Inner Sleeve you must sew. Then they'll drop into the Inner Sleeve; no fear."

And so for quite a long while we sit without a Word. Yet in the end say I ('cause again laughter was overtaking me): "Well, 'tis time for me."

Right to the front door he accompanied me, the which he at once shut so that some Boy would not catch sight of him from the street. Upon finding myself alone, I walk along the street but anon there fell upon me that "Filistria" and now as an annoying Fly flits about the nose, and also tickles as snuff in the nose, so that again empty laughter overtook me. Filistria! Filistria! But 'tis Stupid, Crazy, pure Madness! And paltry, base those utterances of his that I am to put Bullets into Sleeve, and for that Puto Pater and Patria betray . . .

~

But what to do? It was obvious that human force would not make Gonzalo stand in front of a loaded Pistol; and since Tomasz has sworn that he will kill him as a dog if he does not stand up to him, the whole thing could finish in gaol, the which of course I could not allow if I were a Friend to Tomasz. Ergo, there is no remedy (if I wish Tomasz well) save to deceive Gonzalo with the deluding hope for Powder only; yet when he stands in place certain that he has outwitted Tomasz, we, the witnesses, will stealthily load the pistols with Bullets and the Bullets will whistle! Oh no, I have been a friend to Tomasz! If I were to use cozenage then only for Tomasz's good! But the whole matter must be settled unbeknownst to him as, being scrupulous in honour, at no price would he give his consent to such an intrigue; and it came to my mind that as witnesses I might to Gonzalo commend the Baron and Pyckal (the which I could easily concert with) and everything scheme with them, and smoothly so.

Albeit, first I needs must speak with them . . . and cautiously, as the Devil knows whether after yesterday's blood they still hold with Gonzalo or whether perchance their consciences prick (although, lookye, they pressed Cashes on me) and all is changed with them. Ergo, I went to the Office where the duty of my employment called me in any case; yet, I admit, I was going there as if to be guillotined, viz. after yesterday's Walking at that reception what for me here and how will those clerks, colleagues of mine, receive me since instead of Fame, Glory of Great Genius Bard, only humiliation, heavy as if but in a Shirt . . . and moreover with a Puto. 'Tis best, methinks, to put it all on the Schnapps or on the Wine, and so handkerchief to temple I bring, sigh, Walk but barely, as 'tis after Drunk a-Drinking. From their distance the clerklets give me looks but say nothing and only Whisper, and only there together amongst Themselves, amidst papers, as at an Odd bird look at me, and Whisper and Whisper. To me no one said a word, perchance for reason of Wariness, chariness. But there Amongst Themselves they went on whispering, and each one bites the other's Bun, this one nudges that one; and naught but whispers as if from behind a fence. Perchance they were saying that I had besotted myself yesterday; and perchance something even Worse they whispered. The old Accomptant buried himself in his papers and from them as a magpie on a branch gave me looks, and perchance he remembered something of old 'cause he just whispers, whispers, "Merry, ferry, splotchy blotch." I feigned to be Drunk or rather as 'tis after Drunk a-Drinking.

Ergo I asked after the Baron but they say that the Baron with Ciumkała is trying out newly bought Nags. Thereupon I went, and still with the Filistria (for I had this Filistria as a splinter in my head), to the Barn the which beyond the Manège on the far side of the yard; and there I see the Baron standing in the yard, in front of him the Stableman on a Mare, large, grizzled, now Walking, now Trotting, now Cantering or flinging out the foreleg in the French or Spanish manner; apart Pyckal and Ciumkała on a bench are sitting, beer drinking, and looking over a sorrel Nag which was loosely shod. And Pyckal called out: "Liposki, Liposki, where do you keep the horse Collar?" The Baron was shaking a whip: "Halt! Halt!" On a ladder, a sparrow.

It was hard for me to leave the Barn and go to them, and I would even have turned, not gone out, but Dogs that were in the Kennel began barking and so no Remedy: out I did go.

Yet a kerchief to the forehead I bring and move limply and sigh as 'tis after Drunk a-Drinking. They likewise were perchance Ill at Ease with me after yesterday, so presently the Kerchiefs bring, sigh, and Moan, and said the Baron: "Oh, my head Aches, head Aches. Seemingly yesterday there was too much of a good thing but no matter, no matter! Have a drink of Beer with us for, although one may have no taste for Beer, 'tis the best thing after Drunk a-Drinking!"

We drink Beer and moan. Yet those Cashes were grating on me and also I know not how to speak with them. Before Ciumkała I would not talk (having designated only the Baron and Pyckal as witnesses) thus we just Drink and Moan. 'Tis hot and about to rain. Ciumkała went to the barn with a Peg as he had lost the Key. Thereupon say I that Tomasz has challenged Gonzalo but the Knot is, the Obstacle is: Gonzalo fears to stand up to him and not at any price will stand. Say I then: " 'Tis an impossible Thing since Tomasz's oath is such that he will as a Dog kill him if he does not stand up to him and that, lookye, would mean gaol. And also impossible for us not to give to our Countryman so gravely insulted some help in his grave need. And something must be Counselled so that Gonzalo will stand up to him." Say they: "Of course, of course, Countryman, Countryman, and moreover at such a time, to leave a

Countryman, not to help a Countryman!" Their heads they sink, their beer they drink, at me they blink.

I preferred not to mention the cashes for I was ill at ease. Yet say I that haply there is no other Remedy and if Gonzalo would have the shooting with no Bullets, it must be promised to him but hush hush so that not a living soul will know. Thus the Wolf is full and the Goat is whole. Heads together. The Baron eyes Pyckal, likewise Pyckal the Baron, albeit the Baron spoke: "It appears there is no other Remedy but 'tis an irksome thing." Says Pyckal: "A murky affair."

Say I: "'Tis known to me that Gonzalo would gladly have your Honours, Benefactors, Friends of his as witnesses of his since you were present at the jangle, and so we, the witnesses, would in mutual agreement arrange it all smoothly amongst ourselves and, as is being done, put the bullets into the Sleeve; and although this, lookye, an Irksome thing, yet our Intent is pure as 'tis the matter of the deliverance of our comrade, Compatriot, a man already advanced in years and scrupulous in honour; likewise 'tis that Poland's name at such a hard time for that Patria of ours suffer no damage."

Pyckal gives a look to the Baron, the Baron to Pyckal; the Baron agitated his fingers, Pyckal moved his leg. Said the Baron: "At no price will I be a Puto's witness." And Pyckal: "And I be a witness! What else!"

Yet say I: "Oh, hard, hard but must do, must do as the Compatriot is in distress and so for the Compatriot, for the Patria . . ." Thereupon sighed the Baron, sighed Pyckal. Sit they, blink they, drink they, and sigh they. Then say they: "Oh, hard, hard, but must do, must do. No other Remedy and moreover for the Compatriot, for the Patria!"

Ergo, Hard, very Hard! And primarily as the Intention is unfathomable; since the Devil knows whom they really would serve—Gonzalo or Tomasz. They too know not my Intention (and primarily 'cause I have not returned to them their Cashes). But I too know not my Intention and, although I hold to the side of the Pater, old, the Filistria, young, stirs in my mind. But it began to rain and Ciumkała scrambled down the ladder.

Albeit something must be begun. I went to Gonzalo to commend to him Pyckal and the Baron as witnesses. He hugged, called me a Friend of his and, now certain that without bullets the shooting, heaps of gold promised me. Then to Tomasz, whom I told only that Gonzalo had vowed to stand up to him. Tomasz hugged me. Then to Dr. Garcia I went, the which Tomasz as his second Witness had designated: an eminent attorney was he and, having learned that I had come from Tomasz, anon most politely he received me in his office ahead of other clients. Says he then (since in the office noise, knocking, clients aplenty, records being brought in and distributed, and constantly someone coming up and interrupting): "I know Señor Tomasz and am his Friend—but these Records are to be expedited there, and Receipted—and I wouldn't be a man of Honour if in this matter of Honour—and ask Señor Perez if he got quittances—ergo, I cannot refuse him this, oh, may Almighty God—here this Dispatch must be completed—let me Worthily—replace that Folio—fulfill my duty—this letter send off." To Gonzalo we went then and there the Challenge was hurled, the which Gonzalo with great Courage and Pride received in His Salon.

Albeit, when late in the evening and now out of weariness scarce able to stand I returned home, Counsellor Podsrocki's card I find: viz. at ten o'clock in the morn I am to present myself at the Legation where His Excellency the Envoy desires to see me. This summoning as a thunderbolt out of the blue fell on me, since 'tis unfathomable what they would have, what they may do to me, and belike 'tis about that Walk at the Reception or even about the Puto! Oh, why do they torment, why do they not give me Peace! Have they not brewed enough! Have they not induced enough Shame on me and on themselves! And mayhap even penalties, thunderbolts will fall on me for those antics of mine! But since I must go there, I go; yet I think: Bite me not for I will bite you back, and you are not dealing with just any lout but with a Man who will stick in your throat as a Bone. Ergo I go. In the street "Polonia, Polonia" noxious clamor, but I keep going and whilst the Patria's battle and merciless clamour from all sides come upon the ear, I with the Filistria in my head go on and on. In the Legation a hush and empty chambers but I go on, and to me Podsrocki, the Counsellor, came out in pinstripe trousers and morning Jacket and wing collar with a Bow-tie tucked in the "Z" fashion. Most politely greeted me but very Coldly and, having twice hemmed, with his long English Finger pointed me the door. I enter and there a Table, behind the table the Minister, at his side another member of the Legation introduced to me as Colonel Fichcik, a military attaché. A Minute-book and an inkwell on the table indicated belike no ordinary conversation it will be but a Conference.

His Excellency the Envoy was pale and in want of sleep but smoothly shaven. Most politely greeted me, although perchance a bit Ill at Ease he was . . . but naught, gives me a poke in the ribs, says: "Oh, not to know you! You brewed up quite a batch yesterday. You were Soaked, Besotted yourself as a creature ne'r God created, and in front of people, but let it go, so much for that . . . "

Instantly he flashed his eye and likewise Fichcik and Podsrocki flashed. I recognized then that all that Silliness that happened they had on drunk a-drinking put. And say I: "A bit too much of that Schnapps, the colic on't, still Hiccups . . . " Chuckled then the Envoy, after him the Counsellor, and after him the Colonel.

But this laughter not out of will, forced; and belike they would instead undo me. But the Minister speaks: "What say you? With that Pan Kobrzycki, a Major, apparently there was a jangle; and then likewise when Pan Counsellor to the Baron rode yesterday, to see horses, the Baron said there would be a duel. Is't true?" Seeing that already they have news about it, I said: "All that was about a Mug the which at Tomasz was hurled!" The Minister speaks: "Besides, the Baron said that Major Kobrzycki's bearing in this situation was exceeding worthy, honourable, for the edification of all Foreigners present there, and likewise 'tis certain that by that Duel he will not bring shame, indeed as a Cavalier, as a worthy Man will stand up. Ergo, 'tis important, gentlemen, that that Manliness of ours is not hidden under a bushel, and indeed is to all four sides of the world trumpeted to the greater fame of our name, and chiefly at the time when we at Berlin, at Berlin, to Berlin!" (Herewith all sprang up, viz. first the Envoy, second the Colonel, third the Counsellor, and shout: "Berlin, Berlin, at Berlin, at Berlin, to Berlin!")

I fell to my knees. But they instantly ceased their shouting, whereupon the Counsellor put it into the Minutes. Speaks further His Excellency the Envoy: "With this thought did I summon you here, Gentlemen, for a Conference with Pan Gombrowicz to counsel what to do and how; viz. not only with Geniuses, Thinkers, and extraordinary Authors is our Nation glorious, surpassing Glorious, but also with Heroes: so, whilst over there, in our Country, Heroism is extraordinary today, let people over here see how a Pole can stand up! 'Tis likewise the duty of the Legation to strike whilst the iron is hot, and to the divers and sundry our Heroism shew since our Heroism will conquer the enemy, that Heroism, that unbeatable, unconquerable Heroism of our Heroes with fear will fill the infernal forces, the which before that Heroism of ours will tremble and withdraw!" (Thereupon they sprang up, viz. first the Minister, second the Colonel, third the Counsellor and shout: "Hero, hero, Heroism, heroism!")

I fell to my knees. But spake the Minister: " 'Tis why after the Duel—God grant it fortune—I will honour Pan Kobrzycki, the Major, with a sumptuous repast in the Legation, to the which likewise Foreigners I will invite; and indeed we will conquer the Infernal Forces!" This speech of His Excellency the Envoy the Counsellor straightway put into the Minutes and, upon finishing his inscription, being overwhelmed with fervour, he cried: "Splendid Thought, Your Excellency, Your Grace, splendid thought!"

The Colonel exclaimed: "Nonpareil Your Grace's thought!"

Speaks then the Minister: "Belike 'tis Not Badly Thought." At which they cried "Splendid, magnificent Thought! . . ." and instantly into the Minutes put. Having put it, the Counsellor, again overwhelmed with fervour, cried: "Not till hell freezes over will that Enemy of ours conquer our strength, our Courage, and indeed in the whole world there is no such Courage as ours! Your Excellency, and wherefore at the Duel itself should His Excellency the Envoy not be present? Ergo, I propose that not only to the Repast but also to the Duel the Foreigners be bidden: let them see how a Pole with a pistol at an Enemy, let them see that!" Cried then the Minister together with the Colonel: "Let them see! Let them see!" I fell to my knees.

Yet His Excellency the Envoy, having shouted into the Minutes, grimaced, flashed, and lowering his voice said aside to the Counsellor: "Oh bumpkin, bumpkin is Pan Bumpkin, how can you bid to the Duel, for a Duel is not a Hunt. Oh, a silly thing has been said; and how to extricate since it is already in the Minutes?" The Counsellor reddened, glanced at the Minister with the eye of a basilisk but says, yet softly, aside: "Possibly erase?" Says the Envoy: "How can you erase, these are the Minutes!" Thereupon they paled; and all three of them look at the Minutes, the which on the table. I fell to my knees. Thereupon they cogitate how to Extricate, untangle.

At length the Colonel said: "A folly, and unneedfully Slipped out: but I have a means to contrive it all as it should be. 'Tis true, Your Worship, that you cannot be present at the Duel and likewise lead Guests to it for rightly Your Worship says that a Duel is not a Hunt . . . But indeed, a Hunt with greyhounds for a Quarry could be arranged and to it Foreigners invited . . . and so whilst the Duel is in progress we nearby as if after Hares will pass; and in guise of a Hunt Your Worship can point out the Duel to the foreigners and likewise an appropriate oration on that Honour, Dignity, Courage of ours give." Says the Minister: "Fear God, how are we a Hunt with greyhounds to arrange if there are no Greyhounds or Horses?!" To him replied the Counsellor: "Greyhounds may be found at the Baron's and as for Horses, they too may be procured from the Baron's manège—he has quite a few Nags there!"

Says the Colonel: "Indeed, at the Baron's not only horses,

dogs but also Whips, Boots, Spurs can be found. We could ride in a Cavalcade of twenty or thirty horses. Ergo, Your Worship, this or that, port or transport, for the Minutes are waiting . . . "

Thereupon as if on Fire they jump. But the Minister called out: "I'faith, you are mad but there are no Hares, no Hares! Are you Mad? How make you a hunt for Hares if here is a great city and not a single Hare to be found, even with a candle!"

Murmured the Counsellor: "The knot is that there are no hares." I fell to my knees. Says the Colonel: " 'Tis true that there's not a Hare to be had e'en for the taking. But, Your Worship, the Minutes, the Minutes—we needs must somewhat extricate—the Minutes, the Minutes . . . "

Thereupon as Madmen about the Minutes they carry on. I fell to my knees. But exclaimed the Minister: "Oh God, God, how to arrange a Hunt for Hares, and with greyhounds, whilst there is war, war!" Exclaimed the Counsellor: "The Minutes!" The Colonel: "The Minutes!" But cried His Excellency the Envoy: "God, God, but how for Hares with no Hares?!" They shout then: "The Minutes!" Ergo, Head to Head: What choice on't; they cogitate, cogitate, they moan, they moan (and now the Minutes prick, urge, prick) so in the end exclaims the Envoy pale as a Corpse: "Sh.t, sh.t. The Devil take it. Let's do then, let's do if there is no other way . . . but how am I to arrange a Cavalcade for hares if there are no hares! And something is not as it should be and out of this flour will come no bread!" I fell to my knees.

Thus it stood that horses, Dogs from the Baron they would take, and so with greyhounds on leads in a Cavalcade, with Ladies, nigh the Duelling Ground they would ride as if naught, as if by Chance after a Hare they did ride. Then having shewn the Duel to their Excellencies the Ladies and bidden Foreigners, to them likewise Manliness, Honour, Fight they would shew and alike the unmeasurable Valour, Heartfelt Blood, Abiding Dignity, holy Faith Unconquerable, holy Might the Highest, and the holy Miracle of the whole Nation. I fell to my knees. Having so resolved and into the Minutes put, the Envoy called the Conference adjourned and with their noses out of joint (for what they felt they had brewed for themselves) all cried "Splendour, splendour, glory, glory": viz. first the Envoy, second the Colonel, third the Counsellor. I, having fallen to my knees, anon hastily made off.

Only in the street did I give vent to my tempest of feelings. And the Devil, the Devil, the Devil, Devil take it, lookye, now they have a hankering for a Hero, they have contrived a Hero! But I needs must go to the Conference, the which with the Baron, Pyckal and Dr. Garcia had been fixed to arrange conditions of the meeting. Nothing Good did I expect from that Conference since it was already obvious that we sink in, ever the more sink in, till we are Sunk.

Indeed, my presentiment did not mislead me.

The Conference was fixed in the garden of one of the cafés by the river (since hot) but Amazement, Astonishment of mine: the Baron and Pyckal on large, dark bay Stallions approach. Says the Baron: "We have been exercising the Stallions a bit and so came hence." Yet not for the purpose of Exercising did they come on the Stallions but perchance being witnesses for a Cow, they did tremble lest they be taken for Cows, Mares. Soon thereafter Dr. Garcia's Subordinate arrived with news that his Principal in the registrar's office must needs sign a Conveyance and, most deeply for this absence of his apologizing, him, the subordinate, Dr. Garcia sends to take part in the Council. No remedy.

Ergo the Council we commenced; and under a tree two Stallions. I would have given I know not what to arrange all that quickly, quietly and as smoothly as can be, but how, since the Baron, Pyckal have changed beyond recognition, viz. swallowed Sticks and speak very little but exceeding polite, puffed up, Blown up, they Bow on and on. Ergo Say I: "Till the first blood and fifty paces." Say they: "This cannot be, must be till the third blood and thirty paces."

Thus they, being afear'd of Mare, desire this Duel (God forgive, empty, with no bullets) most severe, the toughest to make; and there Stallions of theirs stand under a tree. Ergo, they puff up, Blow up, Wheeze and (although with no bullets the Duel) call for blood.

Besides something Betwixt Themselves they mutter, betwixt themselves Begin. Since with me or with the Subordinate they dared not begin . . . and Betwixt Themselves more daring they did have and, as their Stallions are of no use on us, they use them betwixt themselves, betwixt themselves Harshly indeed one about the other mutters, one at the other gibes. Splinters, Rancours old, older, they recall: now a Mill, now a Dyke, so they look askance, mutter, viz. mutters the Baron, mutter Pyckal, they mutter, Mutter, "Oh, I would shove in your chops!" "Oh, I would bash your bones!"; and the Baron took out of his pocket a Fingernail big, old, broken off.

Howbeit, they could not jangle betwixt themselves for with me that Council, ergo whilst speaking to me, they poke speech at each other. Viz. says the Baron: "I am not a Base-born Boor but a High-born Sir and everything here not Boorishly, out of Boorishness by a pig's snout, but Sir-ishly, out of Sir-ishness in a Four-horse, since in sooth I am a Sir, not a Boor, and my late Mother did not milk Cows nor did she for the need behind a Barn." Says Pyckal: "Who's the Base-born Boor and who's the High-born Sir! . . . I, if so Inclined, begging your pardon, Breeches in the daytime right here in front of people will drop and Do, and in front of people since naught they can do to me; indeed a Jaw I will smash, smash . . . "

Such Talk! But the Cashes they had given me grate on me . . . and what to do with these Cashes I know not . . . for how to return them when the Council is begun? Unfathomable then the Intention: viz. against Gonzalo or Tomasz the cozenage, and likewise unfathomable whether we as People of honour are discussing the conditions of a duel, or contriving a Plot. And if a Plot, then 'tis unfathomable against Whom, and whether we defend Tomasz or for Monies, for that Mammon, mean, oh Sweet, Nice, we wish to contrive everything smoothly for Gonzalo. In this doubt the Baron wished not thirty but five and twenty paces; for the more the Duel smells of fraud, the more Severe they wish to have it, and on all Severity greatly they insist. The Subordinate likewise, lookye, a Blockhead, a Dutchman or perchance a Swiss, a Belgian or a Rumanian, understood naught of affairs of Honour and made a motion that both parties should give a Surety as a Guarantee that they would stand in place, the which Surety was to be certified by a Notary. So everything Haltingly, trudgingly, and the Duel ever the more severe although without a bullet.

Yet over there, over the water, bullets whirr. 'Tis so. If not for all that beyond the Forest, the Waters, I would not this Anxiousness have, but indeed with the sign of that Carnage, bloodsome, not only to me but to everyone 'tis Burdensome, bothersome, and everyone wonders whether something of that will not fall on his head and how not to go too far.

So 'tis. Instead of sitting hush-hush at so dangerous a time of ours, we here this Duel arrange and so whilst there Bullets, here likewise a Bullet (albeit without a bullet). Oh Jesus Maria! Oh dear, dear! And wherefore this? And what for this? And how this? And why this? And what End will this have? Oh Christ, Merciful Christ, burdensome, burdensome, burdensome! . . . Yet no remedy. What to do if there is naught else to do, and only this very Duel ahead as the sole target of our every doing. And therefore albeit, lookye, Dim and very little to be spied, but indeed as in a wood, viz. when someone lost, from the distance a large Stone or Hillock amongst trees marks and goes towards that Hillock to have at least some Target for that going of his. And they are a-going too, every one from divers directions, their own ways.

Thus a-going his was Tomasz, and his Task Severe, Bloodsome. With a shot of his a Cow he would fain kill, a Bull to bring out; a Bull he was calling up with his shot a Cow to ram, the which was defaming his only Son . . . Oh Bull, Bull, Bull! A-going hers was Gonzala furtively skirting by the bushes, sneaking, and now she as a Weasel after the Boy sniffs, scampers, and from Tomasz into the emptiness of that Duel, empty, escapes.

Likewise a-riding theirs, oh a-riding, are the Baron, Pyckal on their Stallions but still they mutter, glance at each other with an angry eye, of their own Intention unsure. Likewise His Excellency the Minister with the Counsellor is proceeding, proceeding on, in their Cavalcade across a Glade, across a Plain, under willows, behind Pines, Conifers, and with Ladies! Wood Dark! Woods vast, aged! Woodland. Oh, Merciful God, oh Christ Gentle, Just, oh Most Holy Mother, and I too am a-going, a-going and a-Going, and this Going of Mine on the track of my life, in that Sweat and swink of mine up the Mountain, in that Thicket of mine. Ergo, I'm going and going and Going and then upon that Target of mine know not even what I will Do, yet Something I needs must Do. Oh wherefore do I Go? Yet I Go, I Go since others too are Going and so we mutually lead ourselves as Sheep, Calves to that Duel, and void the Plans, void the Designs and Resolutions when a man, impelled by others, to others as in a dark Wood is lost. Thus you Go but you Stray, and you resolve, plan but you Stray, and seemingly according to your will you contrive but you Stray, Stray, and you speak, Do but in a Wood, at Night, you stray, stray . . .

But when with such thoughts along the streets I Go, the noxious clamour of newscriers "Polonia, Polonia" not even for a moment ceases, indeed 'tis ever the more loud, ever the more violent . . . and perchance something's amiss . . . 'tis nigh so as if there nigh not so. Although, lookye, dark, nigh naught can be discerned, viz. as in a mist by the water at dusk . . . Yet somewhat I see that somewhat Amiss and perchance is Cracking, Bursting, Scarce draws breath. Thus I go along the streets, go, gazettes do buy, till I happen upon the Legation's edifice and see that the windows of His Excellency the Envoy are lit. The Sinfulness of those intents of mine, affairs of mine, and the dimness, vagueness of that feeling of mine were the cause that I with dread at this house of that Patria of mine, holy, oh perchance Cursed, did look; however, when the shadow of the Envoy's person on a white curtain I discerned, I could no longer restrain that vexing curiosity of mine: and this I must know, viz. how is't there? what's there? what is the Truth and how can it be that we go at Berlin when in the outstreets of Warsaw they do battle? Ergo, with no regard for the late-night hour, the doorstep of Patria's edifice I did cross and by stairs to the first floor betook myself. Mine oath was such that from that man the truth I needs must tear. Thus I go, and Empty, quiet, Quiet. That tread of mine amongst columns vanished and perished, and from the salon the subdued tread of the Envoy could be heard and his bent shadow on the door panes to this or that side moved. I go, on and on, and on. At the door I knocked and for a long time no one said aught, and steps quietened. Ergo I did knock again, whereupon called out the Envoy:

"Who's there? What's there? Who's there?" I entered. By the window he stood; seeing me called out, "Why do you enter Unannounced?"

From the window to the fireside he went and his hands into his pockets put. But anon says he: "Well, no matter, come in since in any case I would speak to you."

He sat in a chair but rose and now to me: "Ah, Pan Gombrowicz," this and that, roundabouting, skirting, between fences, flashes and flashes, and in the end says: "By God's Mercy, speak what of that Gonzalo they say, apparently he there . . . so . . . in such a way a 'Madama' with Men, what?" And to the other side of the room he went, there in a chair he sits, then Rises and at his fingernails picks. I think to myself, wherefore goes he thus, Sits, rises thus, wherefore picks thus, but I speak:

"They say it, they say it, but there is no proof and the challenge he accepted."

"Attend you then lest there be an embarrassment since a Cavalcade we are making and invitations already dispatched! The Cavalcade we are making, although war and no Hares! 'Tis maddening! And this is not a cabaret but a Legation!"

He cried in a thunderous voice. "A Legation," he cries, "a Legation." Methinks, wherefore cries he thus. But by the console table he stands and methinks: how comes he to Stand thus? Then methinks: but how come I to Think upon it that he cries, sits, rises—since when has his crying, sitting, rising become odd to me? And even exceeding Odd; and moreover somewhat Empty as an empty bottle or a Gourd. I look, I watch and I see that in him all is exceeding Empty so that Fear overwhelmed me and methinks, wherefore so Empty, perchance I had better to my knees fall? . . .

Ergo I do fall to my knees, but naught. He halted. A few steps he paced. Again he halts, and stands.

I kneel but that Kneeling of mine exceeding Empty.

He stands, but that standing of his likewise empty.

"Rise," he muttered, but that speaking of his Empty. Kneel I ever, but that kneeling of mine Empty. To a settee he went and sat, as if a Gourd or a Puff.

Whereupon I comprehended the Devil had already taken it all. That 'tis Finished and the War Lost. And he not-a-Minister.

From the kneeling, ergo, from the knees I arise . . . and did stand up. I stand. He too stands.

Thereupon speak I: "So now perchance there will not be that Cavalcade?"

He wheezed and at me flashed: "There will not be," he says, "a Cavalcade? But why would there not be?"

Whereupon speak I: "Then a Cavalcade there will be?"

Speaks he: "Why would there not be? But 'tis so resolved that there must be."

Thereupon say I: "Oh, then there will be?"

Speaks he: "I am not a weathercock," and cries, "I am not a weathercock," and says, "For what do you take me? I am an envoy, a Minister . . . " but cries anon: "I am an Envoy! A Minister! . . . " and thus utters: "You chitsh.t, I'm not a chitsh.t; I am here the government's, the Country's representative!" And now he continued shouting and with no pause as if possessed: "I'm the Envoy, I the Government, here the Legation, I'm the Minister, I the Country, I'm the Envoy, the Minister, I the Government, Legation, Country, and a Cavalcade there will be, will be 'cause the Country, 'cause the Government, 'cause the Legation, and I the Envoy, Envoy, and the Government, and the Country, and at Berlin, at Berlin, to Berlin, to Berlin!" He rushes then to the wall, to the window, thence to the Cabinet and shouts, shouts unto the Heavens that the Country, the

Government, the Legation, that he an Envoy, and continues shouting that he an Envoy . . . Yet that shouting of his empty, and I the Legation's edifice left.

~

But Empty. And in the street likewise Empty. A breeze, light and damp, o'erblew me, but I know not where I am to go, what to do; and when I happened into a café, there Empty the Tea. Thereupon I thought to myself: 'tis the end of that Patria of yore . . . yet that thought Empty, Empty and again through the streets I go, but when thus I go I know not where I am to go.

Ergo I stop. And so dry and empty as shavings, as pepper or an empty Barrel. Ergo I stand and think, where could I go, what could I do, since no Friends or close acquaintances and I on the corner, lookye, just stand . . . and now an eagerness overtook me at this hour of night to go to that Son, that Son to see . . . This fancy of mine was not quite reasonable, and moreover at Night, but with my stay on the corner prolonging whilst I know not where I am to go (since cafés are already closed) all the more piercing. My father had these many years been dead. Mother far away. Children I have none, and when no Friends nor any near ones, let me at least another's child glimpse, and the Son, although another's, see. The fancy, I say, rather addle-pated, but I moved from where I was; and whilst I Go with no aim, the Going itself directs me towards the Son; and so of a sudden I to the Son go (and that Going of mine has become slow, shy). The Son, the Son, to the Son, to the Son! I knew that despite the late hour I could realize my intent since Tomasz with his Son two small chambers in a Pension occupied and, as is the wont in southern countries, all doors would be left open.

Indeed, with no difficulty the Pension I entered, that little chamber found, and there I see, viz. naked on the bed he lies, by sleep overcome, and his Chest so, his Shoulders so, head and legs so, that rascal, rascal, oh rascal Gonzalo! He lies and he breathes. That breathing of his some solace to me brought, but at once Anger seized me that I to him here at night have come and the Devil knows wherefore, to what end . . . and this to myself I say: Oh one must, must needs keep an eye on the Young and likewise chide them! Why are you a-lying so, you idler? I would set you to Work! Dispatch you for something! Order you to do something! Oh, to keep you on a short rein, never slackening, to work, to Prayer, even with a stick urge so that you may grow into a Man . . . But a-lying he is, a-breathing. Say I then: Just to give him a good thrashing so that he would know discipline, grow up in virtue for, Merciful Lord, the idler he is, slug-abed . . . But he lies there, lies, and I stand and know not what I am to do, wherefore came I hence. I would go; yet I could not go for he Lies there and I know not wherefore I came hence.

Ergo Lying there he is, a-lying. Whereupon a Vexation did overcome me. Say I, yet not loudly but softly: Well, hither I came out of vexation concerning the future of that Nation of ours, the which by Enemies defeated, as naught remains to us but our children. May Sons be faithful to Fathers and the Land of their fathers! So I speak but at once the Fear did overcome me, to what end do I speak thus and why . . . But Empty here! Suddenly so Empty! Suddenly so Empty as if Naught . . . as if no thing was . . . and he here Lies, just a-lying, a-lying . . . Empty within me and empty before me. I cried: "For the love of God!"

Yet in vain the name of God the Father whilst the Son before me, whilst the Son only and naught but the Son! The Son! The Son! Let the Father die! Son without Father. The son rein-free, the Son let loose. That's the thing, oh, indeed!

Next day in the early morn—the Duel.

When unto the appointed glade, the which hard by a river lies, we came, no one was there, and Tomasz was saying prayers; but soon a chaise with a Doctor arrived; and thereupon Gonzalo in flurry and fuss with four trotters and a Postillion, and behind his equipage the Baron together with Pyckal on stallions, huge, dark bay, the which with spurs bepricked and with reins becurbed Reared and Snorted.

Ergo then all of us were here. I with the Baron began to

measure the ground but a frog I saw, so to the Baron I say: "Frogs there are here." He retorted: "There are, for 'tis damp." Also Dr. Garcia has come up to me and says to make haste as he needs must for a Cession and a Conveyance.

A sign was given and the adversaries advanced to the ground. Pan Tomasz modestly, quietly, Gonzalo for his part in the glitter, in the fuss of all his array: viz. Sash of blue satin, Vest also made of Satin, Safron-yellow, over it a Waistcoat, black, and a Half-Frock likewise, braided and also Bemedalled; then a Cape in two Colours, likewise a Hat Black, Mexican, with a brim, the which wide, exceeding wide. The Baron with Pyckal again the Stallions mounted, Gonzalo his Hat flourished, Horses snorted. Pyckal to me a-gallop came, horse sharply reined, from horse did hand me the pistols; again his Hat did Puto flourish.

Tomasz calmly in his place stood and waited. I load the pistols . . . and Bullets into the Sleeve, into the Inner Sleeve. Thereupon a pistol to Tomasz I gave but Empty, and the other, likewise Empty, Pyckal to Gonzalo gave. As we were stepping aside, the Baron cried "Fire! Fire!" . . . but that cry of his Empty for barrels empty too. Gonzalo, having dashed his hat to the ground, raised the pistol and fired. The sound went forth over the glade, but Empty. Sparrows there on bushes perched (fatter ones than our own) but they took fright; and likewise a Cow.

Tomasz, seeing that Gonzalo's bullet had missed him (since there was none), his weapon raised and at length aimed, at length; yet he knew not that that aiming of his Empty. He aims, aims, fires but what—empty, empty: and from that clap naught but pop. Here the sun has already a mite risen, has begun to warm (as the mists had dispersed), and here from behind a bush a cow came out; Gonzalo his hat did flourish; and from afar, from behind bushes, the Cavalcade appeared: viz. first two Postillions, one of them two Greyhounds and the other four holding on a rope; in their wake Ladies and Gentlemen in a flurried procession riding, chatting, singing . . . and so ride by, ride by, and first on the right His Excellency the Envoy in a hunting Coat on a large Stallion, a piebald, afterwards the Counsellor and next the Colonel. They ride, ride, and as if naught, after a hare, although, lookye, Empty since there is no hare . . . and so, lookye, slowly they ride by.

Now we at them did gape, especially Tomasz. But they have ridden by. Thereupon straightway to load the pistols, I bullets into the sleeve. Fire, fire. Gonzalo his hat did flourish, shoots from an empty barrel, but naught; and Tomasz raises his weapon, aims, aims, aims . . . oh, how he did aim! Oh, how he did Aim at length, at length, carefully and so keenly, so Tremendously did he aim that, although the Barrel Empty, Puto did shrink, did stiffen and now even to me it seemed that it could not be but that Death out of that Barrel would burst. Another clap. But from that clap was naught but pop. Gonzalo his Large Black Hat did flourish, Pyckal, the Baron horses so tightly becurbed that they on their rumps sat, whilst to me Dr. Garcia has come up and asks to make haste as he needs must for a Cession.

Whereupon I did nigh clutch my head! And presently it became clear to me that we as if into a Trap had fallen and there can be no end here and this Duel can have no ending: viz. 'tis till blood and how is Blood to appear if with no bullets the pistols? But 'tis an Oversight, Confusion of ours, an Error of ours that this we overlooked in devising the conditions!!! They can so all day and night, and the next day and night following, and further on a whole day in rounds go since I all the time Bullets into the Sleeve for them and fire, fire, and so with no End, with no respite! God, what to do, what to conceive! But fired Gonzalo! Fires Tomasz! And the Cavalcade from afar, behind bushes, appears, viz. Ladies and Gentlemen, likewise Greyhounds. Ride slowly, trotting or ambling, first His Excellency the Envoy, afterwards the Counsellor with the Colonel, and they ride after a hare (although there is no hare), and have ridden by . . .

Gonzalo his hat flourished. Tomasz the pistol to his eye raised. Oh, how he did aim! 'Slife! 'Slife, 'Slife, out of that whole soul of his, that Might of his, out of that Rectitude of his . . . he frowns . . . his eyes narrow . . . and he Aims so, Aims, that Death,

Death, bloodsome Death, certain Death, Blood here must be! Another clap. But Pop. And with empty Popping perchance he kills but himself. Puto flourished his black hat. And the Cavalcade appeared, and this time closer, although as if naught, amongst themselves they are talking, chatting, hallooing, after a Hare, after a Hare riding! But now Pyckal's Stallion bit the rump of the Stallion on which the Baron sat. Bit the rump! The Baron did lash him but Pyckal lashed the Baron's; ergo from his Horse the Baron at the other's head, across the head, and Pyckal on the head. The Stallions whinnied.

We to them. But they have already bolted, over the glade run! Off the Baron fell. Whereupon I likewise see that the Horses there in the Cavalcade snort, whinny, and the Ladies fall off. Straightway furious yelping of dogs, Greyhounds came to the ear and crying, groaning—oh, perchance they have fallen upon somebody, are mauling! Leaving the duel, we beyond the bushes with help rush, where horses, Stallions all, with tooth and claw bite each other, whinny . . . and under the Dogs no one else but Ignacy with the Dogs tumbles, by them nipped, pulled! Humans' screaming, dogs' growling, choking, Ignacy's groan, horses' gallop, Ladies' shrieking, men's voices into a Dantesque symphony merged.

Tomasz "A pistol, a pistol" cried, out of my hand the pistol tears, and at the Dogs fires; but the Barrel empty.

Thereupon Gonzalo at those Dogs hurled himself, and did so with bare hands, yet with a cry Terrible, heaven-piercing . . . and, having fallen amongst them, with them he began to roll, scream, maul, tearing them away from that Ignasiek of his, him with his own body, with his own body shielding!

Now also the postillions at the dogs with rods, with whips, with whatever they had; others jumped in too. And so away the Dogs they chased.

Also the horses they caught; and whoever had fallen was now struggling up off the ground and gathering himself together. Tomasz fell upon his Son and, seeing that besides surface wounds no harm he suffered, on knees thanked God for that immeasurable benefaction of His; whereupon to Gonzalo his hand he held out: "Oh, now not an enemy but a Brother, Friend you will be to me since you have rescued my Son at the risk of your own Life!" Anon then they embraced each other to the great applause of all, and Gonzalo's bravery to the skies was raised: "From death he has rescued him! For an enemy he has done this! He himself came nigh death . . . " Ignacy alike to Gonzalo his hand holds out; the latter embraces him and as a Brother hugs.

Ergo, after fear, Joy. Says His Excellency the Envoy: "Well, praise God that it ended so and nobody's fault 'tis save perchance the Stallions' and Postillions' . . . for when the Stallions began to bite each other, the dogs tore away from the Postillions and on the Young Man lept, the which was led by Anxiety for his Father to hide himself in these bushes. Ergo, gentlemen, charming Ladies, you could see the apparent sign of God's Grace the which a son for a Father has rescued.Regard these groves! Regard herbs, bushes, Nature all, the which under the vastness of Heaven rests; and regard how the Pole before all Creation forgives the rescuer of that Son of his! God's Grace. The benevolence of all Nature! Oh, since 'tis certain, most certain, that a Pole is dear to God and Nature for those Virtues of his, and chiefly for that Chivalry of his, for that Courage of his, that Nobility of his, for that Piousness and Faith of his! Regard these groves! Regard all Nature! And regard us, the Poles. Amen, amen, amen." All then cried: "Viva Polonia Mártir."

I fell to my knees. Whereupon Gonzalo advanced to the center and with his Hat a circle made at which the Horses again took fright. He, however, paying no heed to the horses, spoke thus: "A great, immeasurable Honour 'twas for me with a man so worthy, a Pole, to share ground and, Your Excellency, God keep me from such shame that I would not stand up to someone, since I flee from no one and he shall Find me Whosoe'er Seeks me; for I reckon that there is no greater treasure for a Man than the unbesmirched Reputation of his Name. Albeit, if for the reason of Rescuing from the Dogs the Son of His Worship, he, the aforesaid worthy Enemy, wishes to have me for a Friend, I will not waver from that Friendship, indeed a Friend, a Brother of his I would for all time be. And so methinks that he will not refuse me the gracious acceptance of the hospitality of my home, and he together with his Son for Carousing to that friendship to my home will betake himself; where we will Carouse!" All began shouting and hailing, here they Hug, there they Kiss and Gonzalo again embraced first Tomasz, then his Son. Such the Duel's end.

~

Hard that Mountain of mine in the emptiness of that track of mine and in that Field of Mine, yet Empty, Empty as if 'twere naught. So out of all that I together with Tomasz in Gonzalo's equipage to his palace; yet not to the one he had in town but to the Estancia two or three miles distant. In our wake in a Chaise Gonzalo with Ignacy rides. Thus we ride along this track, as if up a Mountain: and there houses, dwellings, many fences, grass, Fruit trees; so we ride on and there Dogs, Hens, sometimes a Cat, children playing and people moving about; so the horses draw the carriage, and we ride rather smartly, albeit Empty, Hollow. Tomasz in silence was riding; I likewise was silent. Of a sudden Tomasz grasped my hand: "Tell me, not to go, perchance . . . for what are we to go there? Since it seems that there is a Reconciliation, seems that that Man has indeed honourably acquitted himself, and from certain death rescued a Son for me, yet somewhat not to my taste that bidding of his . . . Oh, we'd best not go! . . . " Thus he speaks to me; yet empty the words! I retorted: "Go ye not! If you would not go, go ye not. You'd best not go . . . Do you not see that not for you but for himself he has rescued your Son! You Miserable Man, why to his very home do you bring your Son! . . . you'd do better to take Ignacy from his chaise and flee as from Pestilence!"

Thus I respond, but 'twas Empty, Empty since, although for the peace of my Conscience, heavy, I spoke, I did know that my Advice indeed a contrary response in him would evoke, and would make escape impossible for him.

Whereupon he grasped the whip and the horses with a lash did smite so that they sprang forward! "On with ye, on!" he cried. "Even if 'twere as you say I would not from him flee with Ignacy, for my Ignacy is not such as to be afeard of his suit!" And with the whip he scourges the horses so that they spring forward. And I for the peace of my conscience speak on: "You'd do well to take flight so as not to expose Ignacy to that web . . . "

Within two hours before the gates of a large Park we drew up, the which, amidst boundless plains of Pampas, with a plumage of Palms, Baobabs, and Orchids was raised. And, after the gates have been opened, a Drive before us, murky, humid—the which leads to the Palace, heavily gilded, of Moorish or Renaissance, Gothic and likewise Romanesque architecture—a-quiver with Hummingbirds, Flies, huge, golden, Butterflies of many hues, Parrots divers. Exclaimed Gonzalo:

"So we are at home! Be welcome! Be welcome!"

Thereupon to hug us, embrace our knees, conduct us into the house! I was amazed and amazed was Tomasz together with his son upon seeing the luxuries of those Salons, Huge Halls, the which with Plafonds, Parquets, Stuccoes, Panellings, and likewise Bays, Columns, Paintings, Statues, further on Cupids and Refectories, Pilasters, Tapestries, Carpets and also Palms, and Flagons too, Vases Filigreen, of crystal, of jasper, caskets, rosewood baskets, chests, cithers, Venetian or even Florentine, and likewise incrustated with filigree. And one upon the other crammed, stuffed so that, Heaven help us, the head aches: viz. a Cupid next to a Goblin, and here in an Armchair a Madonna, there on a Runner a Vase, and this under the table, that behind a Flagon, there a Column who knows whence and wherefore, and next a Shield or even a Platter. Albeit, seeing the Titians, Raphaels, Murillos, and likewise other extraordinary masterpieces of art, all that we gazed upon with reverence, and say I: "Treasures these, treasures!" "Aye, treasures," says he, "and this is why, sparing no cost, all I bought and here did gather, did pile that they might Cheapen for me a bit. Ergo, these Masterpieces, Paintings, Statues together here enclosed, one the other Cheapening by its excess, have become so Cheap that I this Flagon can break (and a Flagon, Persian, Astrakhan of majolica celadon-green, betraceried, with his foot from its base kicked so that the Flagon sprayed into a thousand pieces). But come, Gentlemen, and let us take sup! To the dogs with all this! To the Dogs . . ." And straightway a little dog across the hall scampers, a Bolognese, although it seems that with a Poodle crossed since a poodle's tail it had and the hair of a Fox-terrier. Anon the Majordomo hurried in, the which Gonzalo gave an order to lay the table since, says he, these are closest Friends, Brothers of mine! Saying this into Pan Tomasz's arms he fell again, then hugged me and also Ignacy.

But speaks Tomasz: "Here the dogs are biting each other." Indeed two Dogs, one of which an imp, Pekinese, but with brush-tail, and the other Shepherd (but as if with a rat's tail and Bulldog's muzzle), together across the room, biting each other, have run. Gonzalo exclaimed: "Aye, they bite each other, they bite! So 'tis. Not with an ill effect that Biting. Mark, Your Worship, as that Madonna that Chinese-Indian dragon bites, and this green Persian carpet that Murillo of mine, and these Cornices those statues, the Devil with them, perchance I'll have to procure Cages for them as they will Bite each other to bits!" Here he burst out laughing and, having snatched a small Whip that was lying on the table, began to beat Furniture with it, crying: "Take that, take that! Bite you not, bite you not, to the kennel, to the kennel!" And in his exultation, again to Hug, to kiss us, and mainly Pan Tomasz but also Ignacy. We marked that that Biting not only from those dogs did issue but was also for the reason of those various furnishings themselves contradicting and with each other clashing. Yet speaks Tomasz: "And there the Library."

Indeed, in the room adjacent, large, Square, books, scripts in heaps on the floor, all Dumped as if from a wheelbarrow; up to the ceiling mountains; and there amidst those mountains—abysses, ledges, chasms, peaks, vales, and likewise dust, motes, so that the Nose is piqued.

On these mountains exceeding lean Readers did sit, the

which were reading all that! And perchance there were seven or eight of them. "The library," says Gonzalo, "the library, what trouble I have with it! God's curse, for these are the most precious, the most esteemed Works of geniuses, of the leading minds of Mankind only, but what, lookye, if they Bite each other, Bite, and also Cheapen from their own superabundance for there are Too Many, Too Many, and every day new ones arrive and no one can read through since too many, oh, too Many! Ergo I, lookye, the Readers hired and pay them handsomely, as I am ashamed that all this lies Unread, but Too many; they cannot read through, even though with no break all day they read. Howbeit, the worst is that the books all Bite each other, bite, and perchance as Dogs will bite themselves to bits!" Whereupon I asked, since a little Dog had just passed, like to a Wolfhound and also to a Dachshund: "And this one—of what breed?" Says he: "These are my lapdogs." The while Tomasz another dog has noticed, the which in the vestibule was lying, and says: "This one belike a Setter, but a meager lop-ear 'tis for as if a Hamster's ears it has." Replied Gonzalo that a Wolfhound Bitch he had, the which perchance in the Cellar with a Hamster must have coupled, and although afterwards mated with a Setter, pups with a Hamster's Ears had whelped. "Wssht, begone," he cried.

Ever the more downcast we became . . . and although that hospitality, gentility of his to gentility in kind compelled us, it was difficult to hide the confusion growing for the reason of the strangeness of this house and this man. Tomasz frowned, scowled, as a carp bristled his whiskers; Ignacy, poor wretch, as if swallowed a stick, naught says but stands; I, although apparently with Gonzalo in league, know not what to expect from this Place which perchance not so much with any rank Oddity but with an aggregation of many disturbing particulars was causing our heads to ache. When Gonzalo, having excused himself, was gone to his chambers to don a more comfortable attire, we stayed by ourselves, but were not eager to talk; and in silence the buzzing of Flies, squawking of Parrots, growling, biting of dogs, in the humid heat of the Evening came to the ear.

Whereupon Gonzalo returns, but in a Skirt! At the sight of this we were astounded, and as for Tomasz, out of terrible anger the blood rushed to his head and perchance he would even have struck . . . yet a Skirt not a Skirt this was! The Devil! In sooth he had put a skirt on, white, made of lace, but its cut was somewhat like that of a Dressing Gown; and a Blouse, green, yellow, pistachio, perchance a Blouse, perchance a shirt. On his head a Hat large, straw, with flowers adorned; in hand a Parasol and on bare feet Sandals or perchance Pumps.

Straight he called: "Hoopla, hoopla, prithee to the table, let us enjoy ourselves, come what may! What ho, my men, serve up!" But seeing our shock, he added: "Oh, I can see as at an Odd Bird I am looked upon but I am not an Odd Bird; and let it be known to you that in my native country, due to the excessive Heat, in skirts they commonly at home go about; so there is nothing wrong or strange in this and I ask your permission to wear for comfort this attire of mine. A Country—a Custom! And I also put some powder on as my skin dries from the Heat. What ho, my men, lay on, serve up, a festivity today. Come on, guest in—God in, with all my heart I bid you and let us embrace once more since perchance better Friends, Brothers I have not had. And a festivity, a festivity!" And Hugs, Kisses and, having seized our arms, to the Dining Hall he hastens with peals and squeals, and there a round table with cups, crystals, Goblets, Filigree nigh sags . . . and straightway lackeys with trays, Platters, Pots, yet, markye, we look—but Maids, perchance! So we look again, but they are Lackeys since with Moustache; but perchance Maids since in Caps; but perchance Lackeys since in breeches. Cried Gonzalo: "Prithee eat, drink, stint you not—a festivity, a festivity here. Come on, gobble up!"

Poured for me mulled Beer; but beer not beer as, although Beer, perchance with wine laced; and Cheese not Cheese, aye Cheese, but as if not Cheese. Next those pâtés, perchance Layer Pastries, and as if Pretzel or Marzipan; not Marzipan though, but perchance Pistachio although made of liver. It would be exceeding rude to scrutinize those tasties, ergo we eat, with wine or perchance beer or not Beer drink down, and although one chews a titbit for a while, he somehow swallows it. Gonzalo for his part was lavishly cordial in hospitality and even a song he sang:

Thine eye that shines so
Shoot quick, he comes ho!

Straightway he cried: "To the Devil, why is there no one standing? Albeit I keep a special Boy for Parade to Stand whilst guests are in . . . Why is there no Parade? What ho, Horatio, Horatio!" At this call, a Boy has come out of the scullery and in the center of the room stands still. Gonzalo to him: "You, such an Idler, why do you not stand? For what do I pay you? Here you must Stand for Parade!" And to us he says: "There is a custom in my country, and mainly in the better homes, that one servant just for Parade stands; but the idler prefers to lie about. Let's drink, drink up!"

What care I for Mistress' squeal,
Pour in, pour on, a friendship seal.

Ergo, we drink. We drink down. Yet hard, hard, oh hard as if you were stranded on a field, and moreover Empty as in an Empty Barn and as if there were just straw, empty. Indeed, in the boundless emptiness of my soul like the grinding of a barrel organ. Howbeit, I look at that man, that *Bajbak* who in the center of the room stands and Gazes, and I see that Horatio now and then this or that of his Moves . . . and so he would blink or his Hand move or his feet would shift or Spittle swallow. Those moves were in sooth quite natural but also an Unnatural air they had . . . although Natural and barely noticeable . . . but I fancied somewhat that he not only for Parade there . . . and, upon more closely observing these Movements, this I marked: viz. that starer perchance does move so for Ignacy. But Gonzalo sang:

Mama, Mama, how this frisketh!
But better still it even pisketh.

Ergo I look, even though as if look not, but still Look . . . and I see that that Bajbak with Ignacy companies and this in such manner: viz. when Ignacy Moves, he moves (although one can scarce see) and indeed as if he were on Ignacy's string. If then Ignacy would for bread reach, he would Blink, and if Ignacy would take a drink of Beer, he would his Leg move; but a bit, a bit, so that those movements of his make almost no sign; but with his Movements responds so as if by movement gibed him along. Haply no one save me noticed.

That very moment a Dog, large, a Setter, has come to fawn; and as a Ram black; but not a Ram it was since as a Cat, large, with claws, but with a Goat's tail and instead of mewing as a Goat bleated. Cried out Gonzalo: "Come, come, Negrito—here, have a Core!"

Asked Tomasz: "And this, of what Breed?"

Gonzalo to that: "A bitch I had, St. Bernard with a pointer, a Spitz laced, but apparently with Cat Tom somewhere in the cellars it must have coupled; and if you were to keep your eye on them, I know not how hard, they still would. But let's go to the salon for Confections as 'tis cooler there and airier. Prithee, prithee, my kind Guests!" Says Tomasz: "Let it be forgiven us but it becomes dark and the way we know not. Moreover, I have urgent affairs; time for us. If Your Worship would order the horses to be harnessed."

Cries out: "Naught of this, naught of this, I wouldn't hear of it. It has not come to pass yet that a host let his Guests go with the night nearing! Heigh heigh. So the wheels I have ordered to be taken off the carriages!"

Whereupon flies, large, golden, with the onset of dusk appeared and under the Palms began to swarm, and after the Parrots' cries wane, other voices, titterings, night squeals of who knows what Animals rise, and the night with its Mantilla covers droning Baobabs. We at confections not confections, chat and do not chat, and although not Drunk yet Drunk, amidst Furniture the which who knows now if Furniture or perchance Vases . . . but Empty, and as in a Waste. And though something is to be conceived, resolved, any Thought, any resolution as stubble, as Straw, as a Stalk through-blown with wind on a dry plain. And ever larger the Void, that emptiness of ours. And that Bajbak as before in the center stands and to a beat with his movements at Ignacy dances, although dances not (since apparently Stands). Finally the host brought us some ease, giving the signal for sleep and calling the servants to lead us to the guest chambers.

~

For me to Sleep the Bathing Closet was assigned, and next for Tomasz a Boudoir where divers Bibelots aplenty, and chiefly little Fans, Figurines of tortoise-shell or porcelain and also Meerschaum on shelves, Console-tables, tables, little Chinese tables behind Screens.

For Ignacy in another wing of the palace a bedchamber was appointed and hence Tomasz's woe: viz. now obvious has become Gonzalo's design to have him set apart. When in the room alone I found myself and with just a lit candle, a dread quite deep did grip me and this to myself say I: What are you doing? To what do you lend yourself? Look to it that it not Turn on you . . . but empty my words, empty, empty. For the second time then say I to myself: Oh, wherefore are you here? Why with a Puto against a worthy Father have you contrived? . . . Indeed, this may Turn, turn on you . . . yet all as pepper, as a stalk, dry, empty. Ergo I say: Oh, why did you slip those Bullets into the Sleeve? Why did you betray a Countryman Kinsman? . . . yet silence, as if after seeds sown, a redolence of emptiness, empty, lookye, empty . . . Here heavy Fright seized me, but completely Empty. Ergo, the strangest feeling I experienced since perchance not Fear but the Emptiness of my fear is frightening me; and not the Fear itself but, indeed, Fear caused by the lack of Fear. Ergo, in that waste of mine, this I say: Go you to Tomasz, confess that guilt of yours, the whole Truth confess; let the Truth ensue here since something bad could happen to you. Go, make haste! . . . yet I see that instead of moving, frightening me, these words as an Empty Bottle or a Chest. Upon seeing then that I was not frightened I became so Frightened that into Tomasz's room as mad I burst, this shouting: "Know you, Tomasz, friend of mine, that I betray you, and that Duel was one with no bullets, for we with Gonzalo so contrived! For God's mercy, flee with your Son, flee before too late since here in this cursed House your Son will be debauched; and 'tis not for you with such sorceries to contend! Flee, flee, I say!"

Tomasz at this cry and confession of mine out of bed jumped and, in Shirt amidst bibelots, raising his arms, exclaimed:

"Is't true that with no Bullets the Duel was?"

Comes up, springs towards, seizes by the arms: "Speak, speak! With no bullets? With no bullets? With powder alone!"

When the Old Man by the arms gripped me I to my Knees before him did fall in repentance, in that Attrition and Anguish of mine . . . but the Repentance empty. He naught but heaved, and this heaving of his heavy, wheezy, seemed to fill the whole room. Asks he:

"So all of you were in collusion?"

"I with Gonzalo."

"And other witnesses?"

"The Baron, Pyckal likewise in collusion."

He heaves and heaves heavily as if up Hill. Says he: "But why have you done this to me? But why have you not respected my grey hair? But tell me what I have done to you that you have done this to me."

Into sobbing then, Heavy, heartfelt, I broke, his Old legs embracing; but those tears of mine void, or as if off a roof drip.

"So with powder alone I did fire? So with powder alone I did fire? So with powder alone I did fire?"

Three times he repeated. Feeling his wrath, harder to his Legs I clung, and not daring to lift my head, the wrath of the grey head of the aged Old man, wrath of the trembling hands, of fingers crook'd as claws, eyes age-old, Faded, and bones dry, wrath, wrath above me I felt. Once more then against his Legs I snuggle, but merciless, hard those Legs of his!

Quoth he: "Aye, let God's Will be done!"

Cried I: "Zounds! What do you intend? . . . "

Oh, God sees that this moment I did all as one ought, and due Terror, Fear, Trembling I shew . . . but fearful to me was that Fear of mine by its very Non-fearfulness. Oh, why can I not at the Father's wrathful legs, and on my knees, Attrition, Anguish, Terror feel, and only Straw, hay, Stalk, Stalk empty! Says he: "I needs must my ignominy cleanse . . . I will with blood cleanse it . . . but not with the womanly blood of that caitiff . . . Here another, a little Weightier blood is needed!"

I to him, to his legs. I to those Legs of his! But hard Legs. Here hoarse voice; here Hair grey; here wrinkles, here a hand being raised, trembling, eyes half lidded and his Curse poised just above me! Ergo I trembled, Stiffened, but in vain did I Tremble, Stiffen, since Void, Void, Empty Barrel and Pistol Empty!

"It seems that I and my Son were to be made dodos; but my Son is not a dodo! And I also not a Harlequin!" And cries he amidst these Bibelots: "Not a Harlequin!"

Thereupon I perceived that for him likewise Empty . . . And thus as amidst pines when Dry, Empty and a distant wind Stalks, dry Plants blows about, nudges, rustles, Mosses calls upon, with leaves, with stems plays . . . and above Conifers, Pines . . . Vain cry! Void wrath! Pepper, wild thyme, and what is lost is lost!

Yet closer the Old Man has moved to me . . . closer has moved, my hand has clasped, and his lips to my ear brings nigh: "Through God's help with blood I will cleanse it, and the blood will be weighty, fearsome, since that Son's of mine!"

Quoth I: "What wouldst thou do? What wouldst thou do?"

He to that: "I that Son of mine with my own paternal hand will smite and him Dispatch; him with this Hand of mine, murder, with a Knife—or not a Knife—stab . . . "

Cried I: "Haply mad! For God's sake! What do'st thou say?"

"I will smite, smite since it cannot be that I with an Empty Pistol fired . . . and so him I will smite, Smite!"

~

In the emptiness of that Fear of mine, emptily, emptily, swiftly I left the room. From the windows of Gonzalo's salons the languid light of the Moon is cast. Ergo, it was certain that Tomasz this Intent of his would carry out, and not only to take vengeance for his being Derided but likewise to save by that fearsome death that Son of his from derision. When in murderous combat Earth and Sky, embraced by the afterglow, on rumps, snorting, sit, and all Falls, falls Apart and Yell, Bellow, Mothers' moan and Men's Fists in clash and clang and in the bursting of Coffins and Graves, in the final agitation of the world, of Nature, Defeat, Annihilation—oh, the End neareth when the Judgment on all living things is come to be—he, the old man, likewise for Combat stands! The Patria's enemy he would combat! And since advancing years him to Impotence condemn, he his Only Son to the Army gives for death or maim. And throws into the balance not only that Dearest Son of his, but also his own affections; that Sacrifice of the Old man being weighty, bloodsome!

But paltry that Sacrifice of his. Not fearsome his grey hair. Vain the Old Man's affection! For he, from an empty barrel at a Puto having popped, empty has become, and perchance a childlike Gaffer and one just to be given some Pap so that he would eat, or children louse, or at Crows, Jackdaws from a pop-gun pop on a summer's day! Ergo, the impotence of that Empty Popping of his. And he, feeling this Impotence of his, would fain kill it in himself his Son killing . . . and, killing his Son, he, by this fearful Filicide, in himself the empty Gaffer kills so as to become the bloodsome, Weighty Old Man, and with this Old Man he would Terrify, Frighten! And void those Supplications of mine! Void Prayers of mine, viz. for him the Old Man by those fearful prayers of mine was increasing . . .

To the Devil, the Devil, the Devil, the Devil, the Devil! Whilst I so with my thoughts combat amidst the night rustling, droning, squealing, yelping, of this house, Gonzalo from nowhere springs out! "But how that Old Gent curses! Everything I heard for behind the door I was hidden! Wherefore did you, traitor, tell him about the Pistols?"

"If you heard then you know that those Merriments of yours with a murder will end since what he has said he will do, and kill his Son he will."

He reeked of vodka . . . staggered, almost fell . . . Drunk as a Sot! "He would my Ignasiek fain murder on me," he yelled, "but just let him wait for indeed that Ignasiek of mine will for me murder him!"

In drunkenness he was babbling. Yet something in these words of his was not to my liking so I say: "You are drunk. Better go to sleep. Wherefore is Ignac to murder his father? Oh, oh, you'd better go, have some sleep. Stop bothering!"

"The Old Gent Ignac will murder! I will induce it since I know the Way for it . . . to Ignac I know the way!"

Gibberish he was speaking. That drunken gibberish of his was not even worth listening to! Yet he had something on the tip of his tongue so I pulled it out: "Oh, what's this way to Ignac that you know? Ignac cannot look at you."

He was offended: "Oh! Indeed, he quite likes me! And I will induce it that he will his Papa kill! Papa Kill—and I know the Way for it! And after he has become a papacide of that old fool, haply my Aid and Succor will need since of gaol this smells; and then Soften he will to me. Tra la la, tra la la!"

Him by the gullet I gripped! "Speak what intend you! What new Madness, Devilishness are you fancying here? What plots with that Menial of yours, with that Horatio are you scheming? What with Ignac has he? Wherefore at Ignac does he so with Movements, what did you with him contrive? Speak, else I will strangle you!" And he in my hands softened, eyeballs rolled upwards, and whispered: "Oh, squeeze not, squeeze not—squeeze, squeeze, squeeze!" As scalded, I from his neck sprang away. "Oh!" I cried: "Watch yourself, you reptile, as I keep a reckoning!" And thereupon he exclaimed: "Filistria, Filistria!" I was stunned. And he again: "Filistria, Filistria, Filistria!" shouted at the top of his voice till this name the whole house, it seems, did fill and on Forests, Fields did strike; and again "Filistria" shouted as one possessed . . . Whilst he is so shouting I began to Walk and then from that Walk of mine—that Walk of mine did strike up! He is still shouting: "Filistria, Filistria, Filistria and Filistria, and Filistria, and Filistria!" That Walk of mine from those shouts of his has become ever the more mighty and now so Violent, so Mighty that perchance the whole House, together with that shouting of his, it blows up!

Straightway I look, no one there. Escaped, the rascal, apparently having taken fright at his own shouts, and me alone he left with just that Walk of mine. I ceased Walking. A hall large with divers things filled but one upon the other, one with the other, there a Triptych under a Vase, yonder a Carpet upon a Candelabra, an Armchair upon a Chair, a Goblin, a Madonna . . . and Brothel, Brothel, Brothel, and with no shame one with the other couples as it goes, Brothel. Likewise squeals, yelps, shuffling of all animals, the which scurried after each other in every corner, behind curtains, behind settees and, instead of a Dog after a Bitch, a Dog perchance with a Cat or with a Wolverine, with a Goose, a hen, perchance with a rat, Flaming, Fevering, and a Bitch with a Hamster, a Cat with an Otter, a Rat with a Cow perchance, and so, epithalamium, Brothel, Brothel and Epithalamium, and naught, and naught and let it go, and on! Jesus Maria! Merciful Christ! Mother of Sorrows! And ahead of me from hence Filicide, from thence Patricide.

Ergo 'twas certain that the Old Man in that tenacity of his is ready to fulfil his oath, Ignac with a knife—or not a knife—will stab . . . and also certain, obvious, that Gonzalo's words are not just words, and that he has a Way to Ignac to bring him to Patricide . . . and so perchance but for Homicide naught to be done, and the only thing is whether that Homicide will take the form of Parricide or Filicide . . . I before Tomasz, that father of mine, to my Knees fain would fall . . . but again Gonzalo's shouting "Filistria, Filistria" sounded in my ears, blowing up my ears, so I from my knees spring into that Walk of mine, a Walk strike up; I Walk, Walk, and perchance the whole house shattering I am and the Old Man killing! What to me the Old Man! The Old Man to slaughter, slay! The Old Man somewhere to reach, snuff out! Let the young one snuff out the Old! Forever is a Father to slaughter a Son? Never a Son a Father?

Ergo I walk and Walk. Yet when I so Walk 'twas as if my walking began to go somewhere and to lead me somewhere (although I myself know not where) . . . and in some place there Ignac sleeping lies . . . then that Walk of mine walks and walks and walks and there Ignac . . . and I Walk, and there Ignac in some place, in the chamber the which Gonzalo to him assigned . . . Now I think to myself, to what end this Walk, to Ignac I will go, to Ignac . . . and, when this thought visited me, I that Walking of mine to the corridor directed, the which to Ignacy's chamber led; and there dark, the Corridor, the rascal Corridor, long. Straight my foot on something soft, Warm did step and, upon remembering the Dogs the which here from everywhere came forth, I think: Dog—not a Dog. Frightened, I lit a match, yet not a Dog it was but a Boy, big, darkish, who on the floor lies and at me without a single word gazes, his eyeballs bulging. He did not move. Over him I stepped and keep going, and the Match burnt out, on something my Foot steps, methinks, "Dog—not a Dog," a match I light, look: a big Boy with feet big, bare, who, out of sleep awakened, at me gazes; ergo I keep going but the match burnt out and again on two Lads I stepped, one of whom white, Hair Reddish, the second smaller, thin, and both at me gaze but say naught, and only on their other sides turn.

I keep going. The corridor long I perceived that here lads Employed on the estancia were lodged at night . . . the which surprised me since it would be more proper if in the farmhouses a porch were assigned to them . . . yet every master according to his own mind governs and Heeds Not his Neighbour's Creeds. Howbeit, from the superabundance of those Boys some abomination overcame me so that I spat, yet methinks: but at what did you spit? And, having stopped, a new match I lit. Indeed there a Boy, darkish, quite Large, a-lying was, whom I, not willfully, did bespit and down his ear the Spittle was dripping. Naught he says, only at me gazes. The match burnt out.

I was seized with choler and methinks: why should you Fix so on me when I Spit on you . . . and a second time him I Bespat. But naught, quiet, he moves not . . . Ergo a match I lit and see that a-lying he is, and on him that Spittle of mine is dripping. Yet the match burnt out and methinks: What, to all the Devils with it, you carrion, I spit on you and you naught, you rogue, you Knave, so once more I will Spit into your craw, into your gullet so that you know! . . . And I Spat but when a match I lit, I see that a-lying he is, naught, at me gazes. And burnt out the Match, whereupon I aloud say: "You something or other, you will not, you carrion, you rogue, you will not outdo me, and perchance you think that I will stop Spitting but just you wait, for I will Spit and am going to spit as much as I would!" Indeed I Bespat him but he moves not and, when a match I lit, I see that at me he does gaze.

Ergo my thought this: perchance he thinks that I so for my Pleasure, for my Delight? . . . And, being dumbfounded, for rather a long time could venture naught, and a-standing I am, a-standing, and a-lying he is, a-lying, and naught, naught, time passes, flows on . . . till at last a jump over him I make; I escape as from Pestilence and rush, dash; into a wall crash, into a chamber or a porch burst and stop . . . for I feel that again something before me a-lying is. A pox on't. Roguery, another one, and no end to't, and flay your Chops I will . . . whereupon a Match I light. Ergo, on a bed by the wall Ignac a-lying is, naked as a Newborn babe, by sleep overcome, and naught, sleeping, breathing. Upon seeing him I was struck dumb, since seemingly as a decent youth he slept. But whilst he sleeps, within him Knavery and—ah, God, a Knave he is, naught else,

Knave, Knave, capable of any Knavery, and were he given free rein he would become a Knave like to those Knaves!

~

The morn of the next day hotter still than the preceding Afternoon shewed itself, and the air sultry, Humid; from which sweat heavy, Shirt wet. Moreover, Sultriness unbearable on the chest, on the mind, and in the bones, sinews all, wracking, the which compelled to constant Stretching, straining. And so we Sluggishly on this morn dawdle, sluggishly from beds arise, with the Host exchange greetings, and Breakfast, breathing heavily, partake. Gonzalo in a dressing gown, a morning one, Betraceried, made of Chamois, and in pumps, in nose-tickling Musk, and his Palm, white, pampered, little Fingers, white, sugary, with coffee offers. Little dogs, dogs divers aplenty . . . a tail if any has one wagging. What given we take, we thank! And the Bajbak again stands and again at Ignac a bit, a bit Moves, and this as if he on a pipe with those Movements of his accompanied him, but so imperceptibly, so subtly, that one knows not if he at Ignac does it or perchance with no intent, involuntarily blinks just so or his feet shifts. Howbeit, so skillfully and melodiously this Jester Horatio aside with Ignac's every movement adjoins himself that naught else he does but on a Flute accompanies. And Gonzalo himself has noticed this for says: "Nicer to dine by wood-music."

Tomasz, who during that night perchance a score of years has acquired, from underneath his eyelids sunken with sight Grey, sunken and nigh age-old at those sports gazes . . . but utters naught . . . and only "Indeed" says, "such ingratitude I would not shew to our Host for his Hospitality as not to stay here with my Son a few days; and the affairs, although urgent, can wait."

Surprised was Ignacy, his eyes bulging (instantly likewise the Bajbak, accompanying those eyes, shifted his feet), but that decision of Tomasz's exceedingly pleased Gonzalo and he exclaimed: "How happy this hour! A friend of mine you be! Let us go then to the park to stretch our bones. Come thou, come Ignasiek, we will see who is better on the Ball court, and Your Worships, elder Gentlemen, pray you, prithee be the Judges of our skill!" A ball from a cupboard took, at Ignac hurled it. Blushed Ignac, the Bajbak Swallowed; yet now to the park we are going and after us the dogs.

The buzz of big, golden flies amidst Palms, bushes, parrots, in the thickery of bushy, feathery flowers and Bamboos, as into an embrace, sultry and humid, was drawing, since the heat could be felt even more without than within. Divers strange animals on the right, on the left scurried off and big yard Dogs, setters, came out with Noses towards us sniffing; but their Noses belike Lop-ears. After Ignac went the Bajbak, and so skillfully, the rascal, so melodiously, as if on a pipe his steps accompanying. Onto a meadow we came where a Palant court behind a fence, next to the Orangery. Having explained palant's rules, the which not the same as for us (since a Ball, from hand hurled against wall, after twice bouncing on the ground, a second time from air against wall hurled and into Bat-Basket, only after two Bounces can be hurled back), at once Gonzalo ball from hand hurled against wall and a second time hurled from double Bounce against wall into Bat-Basket; and exceeding skillful. Ignac sprang and in Bat-Basket on the bounce received it, and Gonzalo at once sprang and low to the ground from Bat-Basket shot . . . whizz; but Ignac sprang, reached it, shot, so 'tis whizzing but just a bit off; swerved! Swerved! Gonzalo after it ran and at Horatio shouted: "You idler, why are you standing about? Better to apply yourself to some Work . . . Such a Nuisance with this Lazy . . . take a Picket and those pegs pound in there, in that patch, for they loosen!" Again the ball he hurls up, Ignac jumps and it from bounce into bounce, ergo Gonzalo aslant . . . curved, curved! . . . Whereupon Ignac makes a jump, slams from Bat-Basket into Bat-Basket, the other cut the ball off in the air . . . smack, ergo Ignac nigh nigh caught it not, and upwards as an Arrow straight; and then Gonzalo from a Bounce! Bat-Basket! Bat-Basket! Wham! Away they wham: bam, bam, bam bam. So it Resounds!

And here the Bajbak aside boom, boom, boom, boom the pegs in the patches with a picket pounds. Ignacy was losing. Gonzalo was winning. In vain Ignacy jumps, runs! Gonzalo, better trained, now Slices, now in Sprints hurls up, and past Ignacy's Nose flies the ball. Bam, bam, bam, bam, Bat-Basket wang, Bat-Basket wham! And likewise Horatio aside boom, boom Pickets pounds. Enraged became Ignac and perchance with one last effort, red and sweating, boom that ball from a bounce; whereupon Horatio boom aside upon a picket! Whizzed, Gonzalo scarce could hurl back! Ergo Ignac again bam. When he bam, at once likewise Horatio to match Boom with a picket upon a peg . . . and so with this Boom-bam the ball whizzes, flies! Again Ignac Boom, Horatio Bam upon a picket, and with the Boombam the ball flashes so that Gonzalo almost misses it! Again Ignac bam upon the ball, Horatio boom upon a picket as if together against Gonzalo they did play; yet Ignac feeling that he has won an ally for himself ever the harder slams . . . And with the boom-bam playing they win! I at Tomasz look, and with those bushy eyes of his Tomasz looks and here boom, boom, bam, bam, bam and when Ignac boom, then Horatio bam, and so with the Boombam! Did Tomasz perceive that this is not Palant but a trap, that with this Boombam his Son is being charmed, that his Son is with this Boombam captivated? Naught the Old Man was uttering. The dogs were biting each other. When the game was finished, Ignac sweating, Overheated, ergo gasps for breath, gasps; and straightway Gonzalo to congratulate him, hug, glorify that exceeding skill of his! And so it went! And naught else from Morn till eve but this captivating of the Son, with the help of that Bajbak this Son's capturing . . . whilst the Father with his age-old eyes anxiously looks on! From morn till eve the same Shame, the same satanic, hellish design of Gonzalo's amidst Parrots, buzzing Flies, as a snake green, large, in the grass, in the weeds.

Since by now it has become clear for what he that Horatio did need. Ergo, we went to visit the stables, and there Mules, exceeding vicious, seemingly like Horses' their limbs, but their biting smacks of Donkey. And says Gonzalo in this sultriness, in this heat: "Nobody can sit bareback on these Mules for they throw off" and at once Ignac says: "I will try"; and then Gonzalo: "Horatio, why are you Doing naught? Take betimes that Mare, over the bar with her, for she has forgotten the jumps." And when the Mule threw Ignacy off, off the mare Horatio likewise fell, ergo the one and the other scrambled up; their bones they tend, with laughter rent, and thus their Laughter, Falls they blend. A-laugh is Gonzalo! Or now with a fowling piece at birds, but says Gonzalo: "Take you, Horatio, a pop-gun, at crows on the slope behind the barn pop for they peck the hens' eggs too much . . . " And so, whilst Ignac at birds in a grove, there Horatio at crows on the slope . . . and again shots blend . . . Or whilst Ignac in a pond a-bathing was, Horatio into the water did fall, whereupon Ignac him by a leg caught and onto the bank pulled. Such this incessant blending, such that Bajbak's eternal, incessant, bothersome accompanying, companying in everything, bothering! Ignacy, although perchance as well has marked what and how, and Gonzalo's wicked design in all this has sensed, cannot prevent his own capers, noisings, with like capers, noisings of Horatio's from being fused into one, as if they were already comrades or brothers. All that Tomasz saw yet as if saw not . . .

But Empty. And though known the fearsomeness of the Affairs to come, though the Son is captivated, all Empty, Empty, so that one prays for Fear, for Dread and craves them as fishes a pond; for more awful than Fear is the Inability to Fear. But we as Dry Stalks, as an Empty Bottle and likewise everything for us as is an Empty Gourd. Ergo, on the third day such Terror overcame me for the very reason of the Want of Terror, that to the Orchard I went and there amidst shrubs that Despair of mine, those Defeats of mine, that Sin of mine contemplating, a nourishing source of Anguish, Woe, I sought to rouse. Ergo spake I: Patria I have lost. But naught, Empty. Spake I: With a Puto I for a Father's disgrace have companied. But no matter, naught. Say I: Here death, here Disgrace threatens! Yet naught on't. On a plum tree plums were growing and one I ate, but a Terror stronger still gripped me: viz. that instead of being in Terror, plums I eat. But naught. Empty, as Moss, as Thyme . . . and Plums on the path I eat, small but tasty, and the sun warms, warms, now yonder Tomasz I saw behind the trees, the which along pathways walked, cogitated, and his Arms raised up, and as if Thunder, as if Thunderclaps called forth . . . but a plum he picked up, ate . . . On I go and behind a bush Ignac lies with his eyes drowned in space and perchance his Thought important, Ponderous, as frowning, something weighing within, haply e'en something Resolves . . . but naught, a plum he ate, and another one. A-buzz were golden flies. I along pathways, lanes walk and plums devour and at Vegetables, fruit look. But someone behind the fence Hisses. I went towards the Fence and there in a meadow a Chaise, in it the Baron, Pyckal and Ciumkała. The Baron holds a whip and the horses are piebald; at me all beckon, whistle.

Over the fence I clambered. Speak they: "And what news there, what hear you?" Say I: "Praise God, all is well." Speaks the Baron: "Here in a nearby Estancia we bought these nags. Sit with us, you will see what fast pacers they are." But I see that Spurs they have on their Boots, ergo speak I: "In a chaise but with Spurs, so surely you are going to ride somewhere."

Replied Ciumkała: "Pleasure horses we have tried at the Estancia."

Whereupon I sat in the Chaise and then Pyckal thrust a Spur into my calf so that I out of Pain terrible, awful, nigh swooned; and they whip the horses and into the gallop! Here the horses, with a whip lashed, as Maddened speed! Here I out of penetrating Pain can nary a move make as that spur had a hooked point and, once into a body thrust, as Tongs in living flesh, affixed itself. I had so little strength that I just cried to Pyckal: "Move not, move not, it pains!" . . . and he as an answer Yelled, Howled, as Mad, as Lunatick, as Damned, and his leg violently Twisted. From which Painful Pain so that a flickering in my eyes, and I swooned.

~

When I had come to my senses I saw myself in a Cellar by a light from a small window weakly lit. In the first moment I could not even fathom how I came hither, but the sight of the Baron, Pyckal, Ciumkała, who on another bench were sitting, and chiefly the sight of those Spurs awful, Hooked, the which affixed to their boots they had, anon made apparent to me the strangeness of my adventure. Howbeit, I thought that perchance they had been Carousing and for the reason of a Jangle amongst themselves, perchance an older one, this to me they did. Whereupon speak I: " 'Slife, men, perchance you are Drunk, say where I am and for what reason you are persecuting me as I beseech, on everything that is holy, that I have no guilt towards you." As an answer just their Breathing Heavy, Weary I heard and at me with eyes Unseeing they gaze, and said the Baron: "Be silent, for God's sake, be silent!" Ergo we sit thus, keep silent. Now Ciumkała Moved his leg, thrust his spur into the Baron's thigh! From the awful pain the Baron yelled out but moves not, fears to move lest the point would go in deeper still . . . and as caught in a snare, quietly, quietly sits . . . then betimes Pyckal shouted and his spur drove into Ciumkała, who in that spur's snare Blanched and Petrified. And again quietly they Sit.

Hours were passing in such silent sitting and I did not even dare to take a breath, a-tremble lest one of those Madmen would a Spur shove into me. I cannot reckon how many Thoughts of the wildest kind tormented me, and in those faces, unshaven, sunken, stretched upon the cross as Christ, and likewise with living Hell burning, the most awful judgments I read. But suddenly the door opens and no one else but the old Accomptant, the same Accomptant who taught me how to enter Deeds, the very Accomptant in person, appears! The Accomptant, a good soul! But what a mutation of the Accomptant! Slowly, as a Corpse pale, comes he forth to us, lips twisted, jaws set, eyes dilated, and as an aspen Trembles . . . yet not less the Baron's, Pyckal's and Ciumkała's trembling, not less their stiffening as in death! A spur he had to his boot fastened and, having come forth, right beside me stopped and whilst no one says a word, whilst breath they nigh seal, I as a Corpse speak naught, breathe not, sit.

Ergo perchance three or four hours we Sat in this way, one next to another, with no movement, with no sound, and something there Amongst Us was growing, growing, growing and, when it perchance up to the Heavens had grown, when larger, stronger than the World it had become, the Accomptant into me his Spur swish-swish! Into the calf he thrust! Upon which I to the ground fell in Pain most awful and penetrating . . . and he Cried out, clutched his head. On the ground lying and feeling that hooked blade the which in a Snare had caught me, I moved not at all lest to multiply Pain by Pain. And again the silence came on and perchance two or three hours lasted. In the end the Accomptant sighed deeply and very softly said:

"Affix a Spur to his boot."

Whereupon a Spur to my right boot was affixed, and he says:

"Now to our Order of the Chevaliers of the Spur you belong and my Commands you must obey and likewise look to it that the others obey my commands as they should. Do not attempt an escape or any betrayal as with a Spur they will prod you, and if you notice the faintest wish to Betray, to Escape, in any of your Comrades, into him a Spur you must shove. And if you neglect doing this, into you they will shove it. And if the one who is to give you a Spur neglects doing this, another one is to give him a Spur. Keep an eye on yourself then, and on those others keep an eye, and mind the slightest Movement if you would not suffer the Point Painful, oh Awful, oh Hellish Point that, Devilish!" And the sweat from his pale forehead having wiped, he says more softly: "Ease the Sinew, then I will remove."

But 'tis hard to ease since first the Fear had to Release me. And when I after long Labours some Easing for my sinews had beseeched of my Fear, with the slightest movement of the Point again my sinews stiffened and a Flickering in the eyes, my skull splitting, Exploding, oh, perchance the Earth and the Sky are bursting! Then the spur he ripped out with an awful Cry, Yowling, Kicking and such Pain caused that again into a long swoon I did fall. When I awoke the Accomptant was not present and only Pyckal, Ciumkała, the Baron sit and at each other gaze. It could not set in my mind that Friends were imprisoning me, and the door was not even locked: just arise and depart. Howbeit, out of the fear that again a Spur I might suffer, with no movement, with no word I was sitting. They too are sitting, till in the end moved slightly the Baron, and straightway likewise Ciumkała a Spur moved; but said the Baron: "I beg your leave so that I can go to the Saucepans, make a meal, as today is my turn." Whereupon the leave was granted him and to the Saucepans he went, but Pyckal right next to him with a Spur; and Pyckal was watched by Ciumkała, who likewise from me took not his eyes. Ergo, again the heavy stiffness came on, yet eased a bit after the food was cooked, and moaned Ciumkała: "Ah God, God, God . . . "

Ergo, I realized that there is no Hope.

I shall not bother my gracious Reader with a detailed description of my dolours in the snare of that Spur suffered. Since a Snare it was, into which we as Rats and as Conies fell and all 'cause of the Accomptant. And every now and then when the Spur eased us a little, from the Baron's or Ciumkała's fragmentary disclosures, from Pyckal's hollow moans I was coming to know the truth.

Indeed it all began with this: viz. that after the Duel, when I with Tomasz to Gonzalo's estancia betook myself, the Baron through Ciumkała challenged Pyckal to a duel—for Pyckal had whacked him on the head. Through Ciumkała, I say, this challenge was, for when the Baron and Pyckal were together coming back from the duel on their stallions, Ciumkała lumbered out of a ditch (he had waited in the ditch for them) and since exceeding angry (he had thought that they deliberately from being a witness to Gonzalo had excluded him in order to thwart his Purposes and him from Profits bar); ergo, out of the ditch he lumbered and says: "Stallions, stallions but Mares would befit you better since you are Mares perchance; for a Mare you were witnesses so Mares . . . " He lumbered up so that the Stallions began to frisk and jump about, and the Baron would a boot give him between the eyes; yet, instead of giving it to him, Pyckal he kicked in the thigh, for Ciumkała sat on the ground. Sits then Ciumkała and there Pyckal the Baron on the ear: "You something or other, why are you kicking me?!" Says the Baron: "And wherefore did you me on the head?" Says Ciumkała from the ground: "Oh, but the Mares are biting each other, so it will rain! . . . " Here the stallions jump about, frisk. Then the Baron Pyckal on the ear! So the blood surges and one the other to a Duel calls out (and Ciumkała "Mares" calls out), and now all the more for that new duel they burn 'cause the shame of that popping with the Puto they would fain rub out. Ergo, when so calling out, at the Office they arrived, the Baron asking the Accomptant in his name to call out Pyckal now pro forma with sabres or pistols. But says the Accomptant: "Why am I to call out since you fear a Bullet as 'tis clear, obvious what people say that that Duel was with no Bullet, ergo haply likewise this Duel with no bullet you would have . . . oh, you Stallions, stallions, yet from an empty Pistol and with Powder you fire . . . " And Ciumkała: "Mares, mares . . . " Whereupon the Baron with Pyckal at them, would beat them, but finally to the Manège they went for vodka. There the Baron and Pyckal shout, make racket, ready with Claws, and even with Flails or Forks, and for death itself, to the last blood . . . and they rage, at each other's throats they fly and at the Accomptant's, amongst themselves poke speech at each other, now the Mill, now the Dyke, and all old rancours, Recollections, all wrongs from the beginning of time suffered as alive before their eyes appear. Then says the Accomptant: "Spurs I have, the which have a point sharply twisted, so if you would with these Flails beat each other, haply better with these Spurs . . . yet these are Spurs not for Mares but perchance only for Stallions! . . . " And Ciumkała: "Mares, mares! . . . " "Stallion!" they cry, and ask to have these spurs affixed and will anon stab each other to death with them! Whereupon the Baron thrust his spur into Pyckal, Pyckal his into the Baron, and thus in a Snare they got so that they could not even move. The Accomptant whitened as a wall, his eyes bulged and, having affixed his own spur, having pounced on them, Pierced them thus, Trampled thus, Gored mercilessly so that as Dogs they bayed with Frothing, and forth to the heavens a howl from that Cruel place did issue. Then began that Passion, Golgotha; that Order, Snare Satanic, Diabolic.

The reason the Accomptant to such a horrible Snare had turned, from his own whitened lips I came to know, when for the night he returned to the cellar. It did not come easily to him to speak about it for of himself he was the most terrified; but this he confessed that when the Baron and Pyckal called each other out, a small Insect happened under his foot, the which he squashed. The squashing of that Insect a cherished Rabbit recalled to him, the which he in his childhood tried to strangle since a Saint he wished to be and for Martyrdom was preparing himself, but the strength he had not in him. Thereupon a Calf he recalled, and as alive, the which he being a boy stabbed to Toughen himself and overcome the trembling which the sight of spilt blood caused. Thereupon a Horse, a Grey, he recalled, the which he was indeed with a spur a-killing in his student years, to overcome Fear and likewise to become a hero and the whole world to save. That Grey to him a Dappled Cow recalled, the which A-killing, A-killing he was till he did Kill for the toughening of the soul (as he liked it exceeding much and even with many a tear over its corpse did sob). Then a fierce Lion he recalled, the which he set alight in a cage, and this to overcome his weakness and for Great Deeds prepare himself. So when this Huge Lion from so many years ago he has recalled, and here an empty jangle betwixt the Baron and Pyckal he has seen, he resolves to give them a Spur: viz. and this so that he himself might, through their roaring, as a Lion roar.

Albeit—how did that Hooked Spur come to be? The Accomptant told me that when War surged and the Clap of Firing, Thunder of canons, and Moaning and Crying and Killing, Cracking, his own gentleness and likewise the Weakness, Smallness of all compatriots became so loathsome to him that he wished to found an Order of Anguish and Suffering, Agony and Awe, viz. that these flames might sear redemptively! "Oh, Potency, Potency, Potency! Oh, Potency we need, Overpowering potency! Oh . . . this is why I (says) twisted the points of those Spurs; so they might in a painful

Snare snatch and not Slacken, so a Prepotent, most Dread Cohort of Cavalry to create the which might Strike, Smash, Smite! And thus in this Order, Dread, Awesome, with those Compatriots of mine I wish to be so as myself to terrify . . . so as myself to violate . . . so as myself from an Accomptant into a Potentate translate . . . Oh, Potentate, Potentate, Potency, Potency! May nature tremble! May the enemy take fright! Oh, to violate Nature, violate self, violate Fate, God Himself violate that all this might be changed! Since no one will dread our Gentleness, Dread we must be! Ergo, in that Snare you yourselves I have caught, and likewise myself have caught, do torment, and will not cease tormenting as cease I cannot . . . since if I were to ease, you would Flay me . . . Therefore no Easing! No Easing! . . . " This he into my ear whispers, and Pale, shakes, trembles, jaws a-quiver, fingers twitch, voice now shrill now exceeding deep.

Thereupon say I to him: "Ah, Pan Grzegorz, what is there here for you? Indeed, it will bring no Good to you, and you tremble, all in a sweat." Whispered he: "Be silent, be silent! I tremble for I am weak. But I will be Potent when the Weakness, the Smallness within me I have suppressed and made to Fear. And attempt not a betrayal, since the Spur!"

And moves his fingers as has been his wont since bygone times.

Ergo Days as Night dark, Nights as days sleepless in that cellar. There naught but Spur and Spur, and so for hours, days, nights we sit and sit and at each other look, and our every Movement, every motion Hard, tougher has become for us in mutual Possession Possessed. Where are the Baron's grace, his whims, his mien? Where is Pyckal's boisterousness? Where is Ciumkała's eternal licking? As worms in this cellar Amongst ourselves we muck, one with the other there muddle; and when after the Stiffening the Easing, after the Easing again the Stiffening and a Moan from that one who in the snare of the Spur was caught. Even when a need there was to do something, attend to something, water to heat, saucepans to cleanse, always in Twos this was done, and very Slowly, carefully so as not, God forbid, a sudden jab of a spur to bring on. And so from morn till eve we Sit, Sit and keep Silence, speak little, and as if we were Enemies to each other, although everything Jointly we settle. And only when at night sleep comes (although there always one with another watched), only then, I say, does our Confabulation begin, and rattles Pyckal, wheezes and hums the Baron, sighs, mumbles, and whimpers Ciumkała, and the Accomptant under the nose or through the nose mutters. Listening then to those ancient sounds, I perceived the whole bottomlessness of that Imprisonment of mine—since perchance 'tis not of Today, not of Yesterday, perchance of the day Before yesterday; and how to strive Today against this which is perchance in primeval Time going on . . . Heigh, Dark Bushments, Dark, Ancient! Heigh, Woods Aged! Heigh, old Granary, Old Barn, Dyke and also Mill on the water . . . In sleep then they chatter, and one with another squabbles, this one at that one Huffs, that one grumbles, that one Prattles something, Prattles, Wiseacres, Wiseacres, till one day arrived the Lady clerk Panna Zofia, by the Accomptant in the Snare snatched, and the same day towards evening Kasper was lured and caught. Evermore then sonorous, raucous nightly Natterings and there one squirms, Wriggles, another "Chuli, buli" whispers, or "klumka, klumka," and from that Speech my hair stood on end and my heart grew faint as if I in the circles of Hell abided.

And in the course of a few days nigh all Clerklets to the cellar were lured till there was not a naked spot on the ground that one could lie on . . . In this press the old returns, and now as if not past but Pre-Past . . . Ergo Pyckal the broken fingernail shewed to the Baron, to Ciumkała, and "Józef, Józef, do not cry," the Cashier says, and the Bookkeeper cries! Or the Crucians again suddenly surfaced, then a Bun, long ago bitten at . . . and again a jab of Spur, again Pain, Torment! And 'twas well-nigh beyond Belief, nigh beyond the brain, and mainly by day: as the cellar's door only with a hook latched, so just Get up, take two steps, get out into the sun, into the open, oh God, God, to what end are we sitting here? Oh God, God, but we all would fain get out . . . and there the Open . . . Beyond the brain! The mind abhors.

Ergo one day I thought to myself how is't, indeed it cannot be, indeed we all here would fain get out, and I will Get out, will Get out, oh, am Getting Out, Getting Out . . . Whereupon I rose, and was going towards the out-let; and they not believing their eyes my Getting Out observe and as if Hope has entered into them . . . petrified . . . Then moved Pyckal; the Baron cried out, a Spur into him thrust; Pyckal, to the ground with a grunt having fallen, would peck me, but missed; whereupon Panna Zofia her blade into me pushed; and so we all on the Ground in Convulsions, and with Frothing!! But what for this, oh, wherefore this, why this, to what purpose, and wherefore, what for, and why?

Ergo Emptiness! Empty everything as an empty Bottle, as a Stalk, as a Barrel, as a shell. Since, although dready that Passion of ours, yet Empty, Empty, and Empty the Dread, empty the Pain and now even the Accomptant himself empty as an Empty Vessel. And this is why there is no end to our Passion and we here even a Thousand years could sit, ourselves not knowing what for, wherefore. Never then will I out of this empty Coffin come? Eternally perishing will I be amongst these People in that pre-pre-past of theirs engulfed? Never out into the sun, into Freedom will I get? Eternally Underground is my life to be?

Son, Son, Son! To the son I would hasten, escape. In the Son there is a respite, a soothing for me! How I did sigh in that Underground for his rosy, fresh cheeks, for eyes lively, shining, for fair locks, and how I would rest, respite in that Grove and by that River of his. Here, amidst monsters, and in the whole of God's world, oh, perchance the Devil's, I had no other Rock, no other spring in that Emptiness, in that Drought of mine save that Son, that Son with sap aplenty. In this Missing the Son, in this Longing for the Son I a Resolve made, the which daring and only by despair could have been inspired, and this to the Accomptant I say: "'Tis good, but too little, too little! Not enough here of the Passion, of the Dread! Much more of the Passion, Dread, Pain is needed. And for what sit we as rats in the Cellar when a Deed is needed! Some deed we are to do so that we are filled with Awe and Potency!"

Thus I counselled. Yet if that Counsel of mine at the diminishing of the Pain or the Awe had been directed, they would me as a traitor with a Spur have gored. But since the Counsel indeed greater Dread requires and for a Deed calls, no one dares to resist it, and chiefly the Accomptant himself (although Pales, trembles, in a sweat). I cry: "You poltroons! A deed I demand, a dready Deed, and one most Dready!" They look at me, gaze; they know that I this perchance out of Insincerity say, that some deceit in this; but likewise they know that if any of them against that Counsel of mine rose, straightway a spur would be given him (since apparently he fears the Dread). And the Accomptant, seeing the dread of that Counsel, likewise cannot reject it, as his own Being Dread he could lose.

Heads together. Speaks one: "The minister to kill." Another speaks: "Not enough to kill; needs must excruciate!" The third says: "Not enough the Minister to excruciate, must needs his wife, Children kill!" Says Zofia: "Not enough the Children to kill; better to Blind." And within the emptiness of this Counselling a Deed evermore dready arises, and the Accomptant, with hair a-bristle, with pale and pearly forehead, a-hearing all the Voices was, and down them as down a ladder to Hell descending. But speak I: "Not enough of this, not enough, Pan Henryk and Pan Konstanty, not enough, Pan Grzegorz! What of it that we the minister or his wife would kill. Indeed, today is not the first time Ministers have been killed, and this is an ordinary deed and not dready enough. Such a Deed is needed for us the which would no Cause, occasion or any reason have, and just the naked Dread itself, awe would serve. We had better then Tomasz's Son, Ignac, kill since death to that youth for no cause given will be a more awesome death than any other. And such a death will give you, Grzegorz, so much Terror that

Nature, Fate, the whole world will piss in their breeches unto you as unto a Potentate!" Thereupon they cried: "Kill, kill! . . . " and with spurs they hack, howl. The Accomptant speaks Palely, empalingly: "The Devil, the Devil, I will not let you out of here, you shall not get out."

Heads together. Speak I: "Get out we must, as here naught more dread we will do; and indeed 'tis not this Cellar that imprisons us but the Spur. If then in a heap we get out, and with Spurs on boots, one will not sneak away from another . . . no fear! But first I with Pan Grzegorz to Gonzalo will go, where Ignac together with his father stays, and there we the whole Murder will think out. For to kill is not easy and everything well thought out must be. And likewise bespurred on horses we will ride and I trust that Grzegorz would with a prick scorch me if I were to attempt an escape or a Betrayal." Ergo they are Counselling, consulting and my Counsel scrutinizing and the Accomptant his nose upturns—somewhat not to his taste that venture of mine. But I cried: "Whoever is a Poltroon, Weak, whoever fears or seeks dodges, into that one Courage with a prick spur!" And cried, Yelped the Accomptant: "I cannot *not* accept the Counsel, for 'tis Diabolical!"

On two horses then, Dun, the which from the Manège have been given us, to Gonzalo's estancia over fields we speed; and the Accomptant's galloping next to my galloping resounds! The Accomptant speeds on! Alongside of him I speed on. Boundless plains! Farness unmeasured, the which a Forehead cools and perchance with a Rifle after Birds, hares, or somewhere in a burrow to repose, to sleep . . . but with us the Spur. And with us that Deed of ours, the which we needs must do. And now I know not whether as a Killer, a Slayer, to the son I speed or as to a Spring parched lips to refresh . . . and the thud of the Empty Galloping, the thud of our Emptiness in these plains of the Pampas and empty vastnesses as a Bell, as a Drum resounds! God, God, how is it that I as a Killer am riding, speeding, how is it that I shall a Killer be unto that son of mine! And when we at a big chestnut tree arrived, into the Accomptant's horse a spur I thrust from the which a Grunt, a Jump, the spur breaks, the horse with his head between his legs Bolts, and that Killer, my Slayer, by his own horse borne away, in the farthest mists of the Plain has vanished.

Alone in these meadows I was. Oh, how Empty, Quiet, ah, an Insect, a bird perched on a branch . . . But the Son, the Son, to the Son, to the Son! Into the galloping then, and the Son, to the Son, the Son, to the Son, horse's hooves against the ground thud! And now before me the Baobabs of Gonzalo's estancia, now a Green Clump of trees, shrubs springs forth . . . but what Thud with the Thud of my horse mixes? Perchance pegs are being pounded somewhere, perchance Linen is being laundered . . . for whilst here horse's hooves boom, boom, there Boom and Bam and Boom, and whilst my Horse boom-boom, boom-boom, there Bam-boom and Boom and Bam behind the trees resound! Lo, Palant they were playing! And, my horse having dismounted, I from behind the trees run, and there Gonzalo with Ignac palant plays and Horatio aside on Pickets accompanies Ignacy: viz. when Ignacy Boom at a ball, then Horatio Bam on a picket, and Boom-bam they slam! Tomasz about the Orchard walked, plums ate . . .

Having noticed me, they hasten to greet, but cried Gonzalo, raising up his arms: "In God's name, you must have risen from the grave! Why have you so Waned?"

Straightway then Food, Drink they gave me, and likewise Washed me since I could scarce move unaided. Thereupon on a bench in the Orchard I sat under a tree and asked me Gonzalo: "Fear God, where did you vanish to? What has happened to you these past Days?" The Truth I could not tell him as in naught could he have been of help to me and belike he would not believe it: so unlike the Truth this truth was. Say I then that, having gone into a field, I of a sudden took Ill; and having lost consciousness and to Hospital by People having been taken, I there for many a day between Life and Death remained. He glanced at me and perchance to the sincerity of my words gave no credence as suspiciousness in his eyes I read. But what to me Gonzalo, what to me the Accomptant's Chase and the Revenge of the Chevaliers of the Spur threatening, when the Son I see, when the Son before me and his fresh Voice, brisk laughter, movements, the whole Body's Blitheness, sprightliness! And a Meadow, a grove perchance by a river, fresh, cool . . .

~

What is't, though, what is't? These Movements, this laughter, what a change in them! But what's this? And what daring the Bajbak's! Since they, lookye, so One with the Other, so One to the Other that almost a Dance 'tis, a Dance, naught else. Ergo, when one a Hand Waves, the other a Leg lifts. When one up a tree, the other up a cart; when one Whistles, the other Fizzles; when this a plum eats, that a pear; when that one Wheezes, this one Sneezes, and when one Kinks, the other Blinks. And such this According, Accompanying incessant, one for the other, one to the other and as if rhyming, such this Companying Eternal, Unceasing with every Movement, motion, that perchance one without the other cannot take a step. And Gonzalo was tapping, clapping and glees so, so glees that loses Pumps and Ruffles.

Tomasz aside plums eats; but without cease at everything gazes. And so Gazes Tomasz, taps Gonzalo, Boom-bam with its sound the two boys joins under the trees, dogs, setters, with their lop-eared Noses sniff, yet Empty, Empty . . . and this Boom-bam as an Empty Drum.

And in the emptiness of the thunder of the Drum, the fruit of Homicide ripens, only one knows not whether Filicide or Patricide. And there in the distant cellar now perchance Punishment, Revenge they swear on me and in the Frothing of torment, Tortures for me implore. Here Flies buzzed. Towards evening Gonzalo drew me apart and, having poked me in the ribs, exclaimed: "Did you see how Ignac with that Horatio of mine has fellowed? How Horatio into Play has drawn him? In them a pair of chestnut colts I have, with the which I will get wherever I would!"

And capered. Yet asked: "What sort of affair—this Kulig?"

"What Kulig?" say I.

Quoth he: "For the Counsellor Podsrocki on horse rode by here and told me in secret that His Excellency the Minister with his guests in a Kulig to my home would come; the which is a national Custom of yours, in a Kulig on sleighs to Progress. The Counsellor in secret confided to me to get the house somewhat ready, some food to make ready."

Here he cried: "His Excellency the Envoy has taken a fancy to dancing, it seems! But wherefore my house is he to visit? I know not."

From the corner of his eye at me with that Eye of his glanced he, and says: "Traitor, where have you been? What doing? Whom a-fellowing? Not against me plotting? But even if you have Plotted something, too late, too late . . . since this very night the Father will fall dead, the Father we will tonight kill dead!"

Under a chestnut tree on a bench we were sitting and, since I was still very Weak, my head against a rail I rested for it was trembling. Then I ask him:

"What do you intend?"

"Boombam!" he exclaimed. "With Boombam, with boombam!"

"What say you, what say you?"

"Boombam, boombam, with boombam, with boombam."

"What do you intend? What are your intentions?"

With his dainty hands Pranking about, he cried: "Recall you that whilom Ignac Boomed, Horatio in answer to him from aside Bammed? Now they are so befellowed that when Horatio Booms, Ignac to him Bams! And now they are so Attuned that it cannot be that one does not Boom when the other Bams! All then after my thinking, according to my Intention! And tonight the Old Man with a Boombam we will strike down since when Horatio booms him, Ignac through the momentum, even though 'tis a Father, needs must Bam. And so he will that Father of his kill! Before he knows it!"

And he ran amongst the trees pirouetting. I, despite my weakness, was seized by laughter and, from the laughter all a-tremble, I cry: "Fear God, so this is how you schemed it? With Boombam! with Boombam!" He ceased pirouetting and said: "With Boombam and it shall come to pass, as God is in His Heaven, with boombam, with boombam, and I tell you it shall come to pass, it shall . . . "

To the right, to the left I gazed: and there bushes, red Currants, and sunbeams through the leaves glimmer. There aways off Horatio with Ignac by a barrel . . . and again aways Tomasz about the orchard walks, plums picks up, inspects, eats . . . I was about to tell Gonzalo, peace with such talk as an Impossible Thing . . . when a Dog, large wolf, has come to fawn and as a Ram bleats; and its tail it wags, yet the tail of a rat. Again then at Gonzalo I look in that weakness of mine, yet not Gonzalo 'tis perchance but Gonzala, and not a Hand but a Dainty Hand, plump, Small though big, hairy; and Fingers Sugary, Slender, though Big Fingers, and haply Fingerettes; and winks, blinks but that Eye of his . . . Speak I to him: "An impossible thing 'tis, impossible . . . and haply you will not Do it as how with Boombam, with Boombam . . . " He hopped. He pranked. "With boombam! with boombam! And after my Ignasieniek that Old Man of his with a boombam has undone, perchance to me Softer, more Favourable, he will be as, indeed, Gaol!"

There Ignac with Horatio a barrel rolled. Aways in the orchard Tomasz is wandering. Said I then: "You will not do it . . . Do not do it . . . " But my words as Pepper, as Stalk and now such Emptiness within me lodged: he has not even answered and only his dainty Fingernails against the light inspects. Thereupon I get up and say: "Around the orchard I will gad a bit . . . " and though my legs scarce carried me, from him I went. He to the Palant court ran. I around the orchard walk and this think to myself: So they will him with a Boombam bash . . .

But Tomasz along the paths was walking and I came up to him; straight though on the Greensward I had to sit as my legs wobbled. We are sitting then on the greensward under a Plum Tree and speaks Tomasz: "Did you see how Ignac with that Horatio has fellowed? Well, much good may it do him! And I here thus walk and ponder . . . but now perchance not for long all that . . . " I asked: "Think you to do what you told me?" Says he: "Oh yes, oh yes."

On the greensward cool, pleasant . . . likewise birds twitter . . . redolence of trees, fruit, bushes, and a Little Insect on a grass blade is climbing . . . Yet speak I: " 'Slife, so do you still in your intention persist?" He answers: "Oh yes, oh yes . . . my Son I will kill . . . " Hearing this, I fain would make some answer, but to what end? . . . And the Boombam resounded again and as into a Drum they wham, and the sound of an Empty Drum amidst trees, bushes, Parrots, plumy hummingbirds, under palm trees, under Cactus . . . Listening to those sounds Tomasz his head lowered, pressed hand flat to hand and muttered: "Tomorrow, tomorrow, tomorrow . . . "

The buzzing of flies, big, golden, and the cry of Parrots ever the more drowsy made me. And this methought: He will kill, so he will kill. He will do in, so he will do in. Him they will do in, so they him. Me they will grip with a Spur, so they will grip. In a Kulig they will come, so they will . . .

Gonzalo commanded some fruit to be brought, we were eating fruit, then supper was served in the summer-house . . . and for Dessert such strange Crossbreed Sweetmeats that as if Pretzels, yet Wafers. And methinks, how wondrous the weaving of God's world! . . . This methinks and the Bajbak and Ignac nigh Together eat for when one a Sip of soup takes, the other with bread swallows down . . . But methinks: Together, so together! Ergo, now too many of these Wonders, too Many, too Many. Let it be as it will, just to rest, just to Respite.

But when Night with its mantilla the earth embraced, and large glowing Worms under the Trees, when from the Darkness of the park sounds of divers animals, and thus this Mewing Bark, or Grunting Snort, that quietness, that listlessness of mine with Unquietness began to fill. And methinks, how is't that you do not fear when you ought to Fear? Why are you not amazed when amazement is required? Why do you just Sit? Why do you do Naught when Running, Racing are required? Where is that fear of yours? Where is that indignation of yours? And now ever greater that Dread of mine, for the reason indeed of the want of Dread, as a Gourd grows and weighs, in the Emptiness, in the Stillness. Tomasz's design—Gonzalo's design—the Bajbak's play with Ignac—my pursuit by the Accomptant's dready Spur and the revenge that threatens—the Minister's thought to come in a Kulig—all this in the Emptiness was welling and beating as with an Empty Drum, and I sit . . . And there, beyond the Water, beyond the Forest, beyond the Grange now perchance Quiet, and vast terrains of Fields, Forests now not with the clang of weapons, but with the still Silence of defeat filled. To his sleep Tomasz did go. Likewise Ignac, Horatio have gone, and also artful Gonzala to rest has repaired; thus I came to be alone with my Frightening Want of Dread.

Then to the Son I resolved to go. Oh Son, Son, Son! To him I will go, him once more by Night I will see and perchance within some feeling I will feel . . . perchance his freshness will refresh me . . . Ergo the corridor dark, long, and I, through the Boys who there on the floor slept, go . . . and Go, Go on . . . and now myself know not whether I as a talebearer of Gonzalo's go or of Tomasz's . . . and perchance I Go on behalf of the Chevaliers of the Spur that youth to murder . . . and my Tread as a Cloud pregnant, yet empty, empty. So I went into his little chamber and I see: he lies naked as his Mother bore him and breathes. Ergo he lies and sleeps, and breathes. Oh, how Innocent! Oh, how sweetly sleeping he is. How calmly his Chest swells up! Oh, what Beauty, what Health! Oh no, no, I will not to that shame deliver you, haply I shall anon here awaken you and of Gonzalo's trap warn you, haply I shall tell you that by this Play they into a Crime upon the person of your Father draw you!! . . .

How not to tell him that? Was I to allow that he, by the death of his own father to Gonzalo tied, would let Gonzalo him entice, and so for ages be in the embraces, clasps of a Puto? But if from the paternal home the Puto entices him into Dark, Black Ways, this will him haply into a Freak transform!!! . . . Oh no, never,

never ever! And I was about to put out my hand to awaken him: Ignac, Ignac, for God's sake, get up, they would your Father murder! Albeit I look, but there he lies. And again suddenly a Doubt comes over me, viz. if I tell him this and out he Gonzalo, Horatio drives, to his Father's legs in tears falls, what then? Again all as of old, as it was? Again then he beside Pan Father will be, and still after Pan Father prayers will prate, to Pan Father's coat-tails will cling . . . Still on and on, over and over, again the same?

Yet the desire of my soul this: viz. that something will have Become. Oh, come what may, just to make some movement . . . as 'tis loathsome to me! Since I could no more! Since enough, enough of that Old! May there be something New! Give then some free-rein to the boy! May he do Whatever he Would. May he murder that Father of his, may he be Without a Father, may he go from home to a Field, to a Field! Let him sin! May he into whatever he Would transform himself, even into a Murderer, a Patricide! And even into a Freak! May he Couple with whomever he would! At such a Thought within me, seized by strong queasiness, I almost threw up, and as if something was Breaking, Bursting in pain, in the most terrible dread . . . since this is an awesome, the most awesome, oh, perchance the most nauseous Thought, viz. him, the Son, into sin, Debauchery to deliver, him stain, him Corrupt, O'ercorrupt, but naught, naught, may he, may he, what do I fear, what do I abhor, indeed, may what is to be, Become; may all Break, Burst, Fall apart, Fall apart, and oh, Filistria Becoming, Unknown Filistria! And so I before him in the darkness of Night standing (as the match burnt out), Night, Darkness and Becoming summoned up, and so him from the parental, paternal home was expelling into the Night, into a field. Oh Night, Night, Night!

But what's this, what's this? Who draws up without? What noises, Sounds those? And there cries, clamour, wheels, whisking of whips, and ditties and outcries. "Kulig, Kulig" they cry! Seeing then that His Excellency the Envoy with the Kulig had arrived, I rushed out to the Rooms to greet the guests.

Gonzalo with a lamp dashes out of the house, makes the

sign of the cross to feign being out of sleep awakened. They cry out, draw up, alight, and with hubbub, din, into the house run, through the Salons run . . . After them a Band . . . and straightway stools, carpets they shove aside, straightway one fell, another a Lamp broke, but naught, stools aside, tables aside, and the Band upon their fiddles struck! On with the Dancing! They dance! They dance!

Beyond the woods, beyond the glen,
Danced Gosia with the mountain men!

As the first pair His Excellency the Envoy danced with Pani Pścikowa, the second His Honour the Colonel with the Right Honourable Pani Kiełbszowa, the third His Honour the Chairman Kupucha with Pani Kownacka, the fourth Professor Kaliściewicz with Panna Tuśka, the fifth the Counsellor Podsrocki with Panna Myszka, and the sixth Pan Worola, the advocate, with Pani Dowalewiczowa. After them other pairs. Throng! Throng! And perchance the flower of that Colony of ours! All pairs! In a flock they came and in a flock they Dance, hoopla, hoopla, fiddle dee dee, heels they spark, the whole House fill so that into the Park it bursts. Chirp, chirp, chirp, with his children in a chimney Mazur-cricket sits! And in the lake all the fishes are a-sleeping! Kulig now, Kulig!

Caught Pan Zenon Panna Ludka, Whirled:

Beyond the wood, beyond the glen,
Danced Gosia with the mountain men!

Here servants rush about with food, with bottles, tables lay, there Gonzalo gives commands, and coachmen, footmen peer through windows, and now the whole house Booms so that into Meadows, into Fields is booming out! Let's drink! Let's revel, have a drink, why do you not? And Another! Hoopla, hoopla, heigh, heigh, heigh! Ooh, Panna Zosia! Ooh, Panna Małgosia! And what there, Pan Szymon? Hey, Pan Mateusz, it's been years! Here today, gone tomorrow! Yet to me Panna Muszka and Panna Tolcia run up: "Dance! Dance! Kulig!" And fervent, fervid, they smile and Sing.

Now say I to Counsellor Podsrocki who beside me a Bottle was opening: "Fear God, perchance some good News has come the which I know not, as such extraordinary jubilance of all Compatriots led by the Envoy himself cannot be for any other reason save victory over the enemy. Yet I in gazettes have read that all is over and our loss." To me he replied: "Be silent, be Silent. Indeed massacre, defeat, the end; now our backs to the wall! But we with His Excellency the Envoy contrived to shew naught, but indeed with a Kulig, with a Kulig! Pawn all, but give a ball."

Pawn all, but give a ball.

Pawn all, but give a ball.

And straightway a mug he raises: "Vivat! Vivat!" "Vivat!"—they shout, and the dancers as a serpent through all the halls snake, and with Shaking, heel-sparking and with stamping, with clapping! Now into pairs they broke and in Pairs they dance! And there aside the elders prattling, Pouring, or else cordially kissing: Oh, Pan Walenty, oh, Pan Franciszek, and what of Pani Doktorowa, and how are the Children? Another drop! God reward you, God reward you! But the Minister pounced on me: "Dance, you Milksop, why dance you not? Know you not that a dance suits the soles of a Pole as a Prayer becometh his soul?" Dance, dance, a Krakowian dance!

We're not just a crowd
But Krakowians proud!

Say I to him: "I would dance, but apparently all is lost!"

Flashed his eye to the right and to the left. "Be silent! Be silent! Put away what you are saying as people will take us for naught! Have you gone silly to flaunt it! Pawn all, but give a ball."

Pawn all, but give a ball.

Pawn all, but give a ball.

More, more, more! On and on! Dance, dance! And shew the Foreigners how we dance! And dance, dance! And shew what those Songs of ours, what our capers, what bestamping! Shew what those Girls of ours, what Boys we have! Blood, not water! More,

more, more! And may they see what that Beauty of ours! Oberek, Mazur, Mazur!

The soul of a Mazur so sticketh
That when he is dead he still kicketh!

Dance, dance, dance! . . . To my knees I did fall. But old Pan Kaczeski has beckoned me, viz. for the need he would go out and lest Dogs pounce on him . . . Then along with him outside I went and, whilst he under a bush is relieving himself, I at the house glance the which into Fields, into Forests with dance and with light and with boisterous Festivity booms. And above the Sky black, as if Drooping. And here the Kulig roars, and Charms, and now Loves, with itself in Love as Enchanted, and Loves, Loves, and Litheness, Swagger, and with heels they spark and in Love with, in Love with, in Love, with itself Enamoured, and in Love, so let's Love One Another, Love One Another! More, more, more! Oh, the Loving and Loving and Loving . . . And the sky black, empty; and here nearby a bush dark, inscrutable . . . and further two trees stood . . . and further a mound was but Dark, Immovable . . .

And something there beyond the bushes, not far from the fence, has Rustled. I look and there a strange Creature slipped away clumsily: a calf not a calf, a Dog large but with hooves and as if hunchbacked. The bush I parted and I see that under the Magnolias a similar creature bounds, and indeed as if someone bareback on a Dog rode: but two human heads has! As soon as I saw two human heads I felt my skin benumbed and my first desire to flee into the House; yet I refrained and resolved to scrutinize this impurity.

Sidling then along the fence, beyond the Bushes, I skirt: and there rustling, hopping and as if horses . . . since heavily they hop, groan. And also Heaving but as if Human. And now as if a Grunt quiet, Stifled, or kicking or Treading. And perchance quite a number, although not Dogs, not Horses, likewise not People. Closer still amidst the bushes I went till in the murkiness, some fifty steps away, a large Heap I saw . . . Since as a Heap it stood behind the trees, and as if Hopped, as if Randy, as if with Tooth and claw, yet

Restrained, as if on the spot with Hooves stamped . . . and Snorting, grunting, quiet, stifled, or perchance a Groan and nigh human . . . Thus this sight so Painful and so Awesome, Dreadsome, so O'erdreadsome, that into a pillar of salt I turned and as if frozen could not move.

Now one of these creatures in clumsy hops came closer to me (and indeed as a rider on a horse, the which when exercising a horse with a spur Trains it and with a bit restrains it)—and the Baron it was! The Baron on Ciumkała! And anon another Horseman rode up in whom the Accomptant I recognized: he, heavily Tramping, on Cieciszowski sat and him with a spur pinched and with a bit restrained, so that Cieciszowski snorted, grunted! Rasped then the Accomptant quietly, Fearsomely: "Everything ready?" "Ready," rasped the Baron fearsomely. "Not yet!" rasped the Accomptant with fear. "We are not Dread enough yet! Still more Spur to our Horses! Let them bolt! And only when that Cavalry of ours becomes arch-hellish will I give a sign to attack, and we will Strike! And after we Strike, we will Trample! And after we trample, we will Expunge! And we will Vanquish, Vanquish!"

"We will vanquish!" rasped Ciumkała with a grunt, with a black rasp. "We will vanquish for we are Dread, Dread. Oh, Strike, Kill, Awe, Awe, Mount, Mount! Strike, Kill," they rasped. "Strike-Kill!"

Hearing these words, the which in the night quietude of the park as mad sounded, I made a jump and through the bushes to the house ran, and the door behind me as on Pestilence I shut. God, God, God . . .

But there needs be a warning so that doors, windows they would close, to arms, to arms! Oh, Hell-hounds! But what's this, what's this? What is this Sound that Resounds? Now I look: All pairs are dancing! More, more, more! Likewise dances Ignacy, with Panna Tuśka he dances, and so briskly, gallantly turns, so bravely swirls that she in his hands whirrs . . . and so amazed are the Old that they give him applause . . . Yet when he Stamps someone there Stamps, and likewise when he Jumps someone Jumps . . . And no one else perchance that was but Horatio who for the dance Panna Muszka took and so swiftly Swirls, Twists that she whirrs, whirrs, whirrs! Ergo, the twain Tap, Stamp, Turn now right now left, Twist so that as tops their misses! Oh, they are dancing, dancing! And when Ignac jumps, Horatio Jumps, when Horatio tramps, Ignac stamps. Bang! And boom, and bam boom, and bam bam boom bam! Boombam, Boombam, Boombam, bam, bam, boom, boom, in a Boombam they dance!

In a Boombam! Boombam's voice as a Drum ever stronger sounds! Gonzalo in a black Mantilla-cloak, like a Hat, twice through the whole hall passed and with his applause the dancers he honoured. And I, hearing the Boombam's call, my head lowered and my eyelids lowered somewhat . . . and now so Empty, Empty that as a Drum empty! . . . But the Minister sprang at me: "By God!" he cries, "what's this! Perchance they have Besotted themselves! To the Devil with such a Dance, indeed now they drown out the Music so they should be taken by the scruff and thrown out! . . . " But Ignac Boomed, whereupon Horatio Bammed, Bam, Bam, Boom, Boom, so that window panes shudder and cups and likewise saucers jump, so that the floor groans! Other dancers there still tried to dance, to complement, as this is a Kulig, a Kulig, Mazurka, Mazurka, but not a chance! No more a Kulig, just Boombam, Boombam, and in a corner they have gathered, they see and they hear Boom, Boom, Boom, Bam, Bam, Boombam as a Horse thunders! Tomasz a long knife took, the which for cutting Meat, and as if would cut Meat . . . yet into a jacket's pocket dropped the knife . . .

So fain would I cry Filicide, Filicide! Yet Patricide! As now in Jumps, Stamps, Boom, bam Ignac unbound in boom with Horatio out-booming booms, booms, booms! Boom into a Lamp Horatio, Bam into a lamp Ignacy, but Boom bam Horatio into a vase, Ignacy bam into a vase; and boom Horatio into Tomasz!

God! Tomasz to the ground fell! . . .

Tomasz to the ground fell! . . . And here Bam, bam Ignac with his Bam swoops, oh, and he will Bam, bam into that Father of his, he will Bam, oh likewise he will Bam, Bam . . .

Oh Son, Son, Son! May the Father die! The Son's the thing, oh indeed! And the Devil, the Devil, and the Devil, perchance the Devil, let the Devil, the Devil, oh the Devil, the Devil, the Devil, Bam the Devil, Boom the Devil! Swoops Ignac! Let what is to become become! Let it Be! Let Son murder Father! And now in this Sin, mortal, common, in this Shame, in this lechery, naught but the Boombam's call and the Galloping of the arch-hellish cavalry and the thunder of a Murder! And a shame before People!

A shame before People, a shame! Since 'tis, lookye, as if Barefoot, in breeches, and as if you had a Shirt between the teeth, as if you a Turnip, raw, a Carrot bite, as if you somewhere behind a Barn relieved yourself, and as if Naked along a field you ran, and as if an Oaf, and as if you scratched yourself behind the ear, and a shame, a shame, a shame as in a Shirt! Oh, oh! a shame before people! Oh God, God, the Devil, the Devil, but indeed he is now Swooping, Swooping, likewise now he will that Father of his bam, will bam with that bam of his, him will Bam! Jesus, Maria, Jesus, and what shame, bitter, nagging, and what Shame there will be, indeed he will him bam, bam, bam! But what's this, what's this? Oh, perchance Salvation! Oh what's this, how's this, what's this? Ah, perchance Salvation! Since, whilst he so at his Father Swoops, Swoops, Swoops, and yet Swoops, is Swooping, nigh, nigh Swooping down, upon him Laughter, oh, on him Laughter, Laughter, God, God, he into Laughter perchance, oh, he into Laughter and so he into Laughter, into Laughter is Swooping and aloft he Swoops! Ah, aloft Swoops! Laughter then, Laughter! The Minister his belly clutched, with laughter bammed! And Boom, Bam, Pyckal the Baron by the belly clutched, and the Accomptant Cieciszowski clutched, and with Laughter they boomed, bammed, Bam, Bam; there the Elders titter so they Totter, here Pani Dowalewiczowa squeals, tears sheds, squeals and Bam, Boom roars; Spits, snorts from laughter the reverend Parson, and Muszka and Tuśka so Skip about now their noses are besnotted! Laughter then Boomed! Totters Chairman Pucek! And by the wall they Gasp, well-nigh Piss, and there again Stifle, now perchance Can no more; here again one from laughter a Stitch so in Stitches, or Chokes and indeed through his ears sprays, there again on the floor another sat, his legs stretched out, and Soars, Roars with laughter shaking, quaking and Shakes, shakes . . . And another even swelled with that Swelling! So they Boom! Thereupon somewhat quietened. Then again now this, now that, first one, whereupon another, and presently three, four, presently five Bam, Boom with laughter Boom, Boom Out, into arms each other take, Totter, now lightly, now heavily together they Pitch and now one the other, one with the other but Boom boom oh Guffaw, Guffaw so much that perchance they Boom. And so from Laughter into Laughter, they with laughter Boom, with laughter bam, boom, boom, bam Boom! . . .